Infer

"*Infernal Affairs* has eve[...]r-
mal mystery genre, and [...]*n*

"Filled with snark, wit, emotion, and charm."
—DangerousRomance.com

"A good read." —*Night Owl Reviews*

Inhuman Resources

"I love this series with a passion, and *Inhuman Resources* is def-
initely my favorite thus far . . . I love the juxtaposition of modern
science (verging on the futuristic sometimes) and weird magic."
—*The Green Man Review*

"A truly enjoyable urban fantasy filled with magic, romance,
and crime fighting that pits semihuman Tess Corday against
all that goes bump in the night." —*Smexy Books*

"For people who like *CSI* and its ilk, *Inhuman Resources* is a
good urban fantasy version of the forensic genre. And for all
the detecting urban fantasy heroines do, it's fun to read about
one who actually is a member of the magical law enforcement."
—*The Good, The Bad and The Unread*

A Flash of Hex

"Wonderfully detailed, easily visualized, and overflowing in
paranormal crime scene action. The aspect most likely to cap-
ture the reader's attention is the author's talent in developing
charming characters who are passionate in both their professional and personal lives." —*Darque Reviews*

continued . . .

Bleeding Out

Jes Battis

ACE BOOKS, NEW YORK

THE BERKLEY PUBLISHING GROUP
Published by the Penguin Group
Penguin Group (USA) Inc.
375 Hudson Street, New York, New York 10014, USA

Penguin Group (Canada), 90 Eglinton Avenue East, Suite 700, Toronto, Ontario M4P 2Y3, Canada
(a division of Pearson Penguin Canada Inc.) • Penguin Books Ltd., 80 Strand, London WC2R 0RL,
England • Penguin Group Ireland, 25 St. Stephen's Green, Dublin 2, Ireland (a division of Penguin
Books Ltd.) • Penguin Group (Australia), 250 Camberwell Road, Camberwell, Victoria 3124, Australia
(a division of Pearson Australia Group Pty. Ltd.) • Penguin Books India Pvt. Ltd., 11 Community
Centre, Panchsheel Park, New Delhi—110 017, India • Penguin Group (NZ), 67 Apollo Drive,
Rosedale, Auckland 0632, New Zealand (a division of Pearson New Zealand Ltd.) • Penguin Books
(South Africa) (Pty.) Ltd., 24 Sturdee Avenue, Rosebank, Johannesburg 2196, South Africa

Penguin Books Ltd., Registered Offices: 80 Strand, London WC2R 0RL, England

BLEEDING OUT

An Ace Book / published by arrangement with the author

PUBLISHING HISTORY
Ace mass-market edition / June 2012

Copyright © 2012 by Jes Battis.
Cover art by Timothy Lantz.
Cover design by Lesley Worrell.
Interior text design by Laura K. Corless.

ISBN: 978-1-937007-63-8

ACE
Ace Books are published by The Berkley Publishing Group,
a division of Penguin Group (USA) Inc.,
375 Hudson Street, New York, New York 10014.
ACE and the "A" design are trademarks of Penguin Group (USA) Inc.

PRINTED IN THE UNITED STATES OF AMERICA

10 9 8 7 6 5 4 3 2 1

ALWAYS LEARNING   PEARSON

For Rowan

———

In the golden lightning
Of the sunken sun,
O'er which clouds are bright'ning,
Thou dost float and run,
Like an unbodied joy whose race is just begun.

—"To a Skylark," Percy Bysshe Shelley

Acknowledgments

It's hard to close a series. You don't want to say good-bye to the characters, even when you know that they're late for new adventures and you have to say good-bye. I will certainly miss writing about this peculiar family, but I also feel that they can take care of themselves, as they have taken care of me.

I owe a lot to my friends and family, who call me to make sure I'm alive whenever I'm in the middle of finishing a book. Medrie, Mark, and Rowan, thank you for always letting me come over and play. Bea, thanks for the dirty talk. Mom, thanks for sending me books. Dad, thanks for the cauldron. Manuel, thanks for convincing me to take the *teleférico*. Madrid, *te amo y te agradezco*. Vancouver, thanks for everything.

Very young, I would take my mother's Meteor and drive into the desert. There I spent entire days, nights, dawns. Driving fast and then slowly, spinning out the light in its mauve and small lines which like veins mapped a great tree of life in my eyes.

—*Mauve Desert*, Nicole Brossard

I

Nobody speaks until we see the headlights. Then a ripple of energy passes through the dark room. I raise my hand for silence. The van idles for a bit in the drive-way, then stops. For a moment there's nothing more. Then the door of the van opens. Derrick looks at me. I nod. He and Miles cross the room and take up position on either side of the entrance. Now there are footsteps. I breathe. I'm suddenly riven. What if this is a bad idea? What if it goes horribly wrong?

I hear the key. By now, I really should be past worry-ing about things going horribly wrong. I should be past fun-sized candy, too, but I'm not.

The door opens.

A figure pauses at the entrance. It could be a midnight

letter carrier, or a vampire Girl Scout. But I know better. I smile. I've been waiting for this moment for years, ever since he told me how old he was.

"Now."

Derrick turns on the light. I raise my hands in the air. We raise our voices and scream at him:

"*¡Cumpleaños feliz!*"

For a second, all Lucian can do is stare at us in shock. We're all wearing pointed hats, even Derrick. Mia and Patrick hold noisemakers, but seem loath to use them. A streamer falls quietly from the ceiling.

I step forward.

"Happy ninety-first birthday, Lucian."

"When you put it that way, I feel as if my body should actually be decaying."

"But it's not. And I'm thankful for that."

"You looked really surprised," Derrick says. "For one second, I thought you might actually kill us all with necromancy."

"Have I ever once tried to do that?"

"No. But in our line of work, you have to be prepared."

Lucian turns to me. "So that's why you kept sending me on errands today. You were plotting something fierce."

"Well, I don't want to brag. There is punch, though, and possibly Mad Libs."

"Thanks."

"All right," Derrick says. "Let's party like it's the twenties."

"Can we stop referencing my age, please?"

"Fine. Let's party like the mystical badasses that we are."

Lucian has an odd expression on his face, like uncertain delight. "Still, it's just another birthday. There's no need to bring the house down. I'm touched that you guys went to all this trouble, but—"

Mia hands him a glass of punch. "Lucian, you're a creepy old man, and we need to celebrate that. Derrick bought an ice-cream cake."

Lucian looks at him. "Dude, seriously?"

"It's in the kitchen. Want to see it?"

"I think I do."

The kitchen is full of brass light. Derrick's herbs have perked up in their bottles. Outside, our neighbor is smoking menthols, and I ignore the tickle in my throat. As per instructions laid out by Mia and Patrick, there is a frosted necromancer on the white face of the cake.

Lucian frowns slightly. "This is me?"

"No, it's an everynecromancer," Mia says.

"Is the everynecromancer holding someone's arm?"

"Of course. Dead bodies are your power source."

"I told you he wasn't going to get it," Patrick says. "For the record, man, I wanted you to be holding a fudge pitchfork."

"Why would I be doing that?"

I put my arm around him. "Just suck in the love and cut the cake, darling."

It's patio season, festival season, the British Columbia summer that's always gently nudging you in the direction of a bar. Beyond our house, Commercial Drive simmers with the intensity of grad student drinking. As Lucian gently cuts through his ice-cream icon, I remember what it felt like to kill him. He had ceased to exist in front of me. Now he was grabbing a fork, and I couldn't help but wonder if we were all sharing frozen dessert with a dead person.

Okay, I'd said to him once. *So you're basically an undead plant.*

I don't like that term.

A zombie plant?

Tess.

Just explain it to me. It's a part of you I'd like to know more about.

But he hadn't explained it. He'd kissed me.

As soon as the cake is gone, the shot glasses come out. Derrick unwraps a bottle of *grappamiel* from Uruguay. He raises his own shot glass in a toast.

"Lucian, you are a part of this family. You've saved our asses many times in the past, and you gave me the gift of *panqueques con dulce de leche. ¡Cumpleaños feliz!*"

The dancing lasts for only about ten minutes, since nobody but Lucian can actually dance. Miles has some sweet moves until his hearing aids run out of juice. Mia brings in Bits 'n Bites, and suddenly it's just a regular evening with all of us sitting in the living room, competing for attention. Patrick tells us about a vampire who was recently found guilty of dealing blood Popsicles. Like many of his stories, this one ends in public immolation. As Magnate, he oversees vampire justice in Vancouver, which is a lot of responsibility for a kid. Judging from his most recent transcripts—which, obviously, I should not have looked at—most of his legacy is being spent on beer and graphic novels.

The air dampens, and we're pulled outside. Mia drags out a box full of cards, and we play Canadian Trivial Pursuit for dummies, which means that any historical question answered by anyone is considered a patriotic victory. Mia racks up points. A dozen universities already want her, but she refuses to make a decision. My heart seizes at the thought of her leaving home. I know she's not my kid, I know that nothing genetic binds us, but she's my water, my blood, my very breath. We bought this house so that she could have something close to a normal life. Who will we be without her? Patrick barely needs us at this point, and even though he hasn't said anything, I know that Derrick would like to move in with Miles. Any sane person would.

I look at Lucian. I love him, but I'm not moving to Yaletown. Suddenly, I imagine myself living alone in the house, and it's hard to breathe. I don't need all this space. It will only attract ghosts, or worse.

I stand up. "I'm going to the store for cigarettes and chips."

"We also need Brillo Pads," Derrick says.

"I can't promise anything."

Lucian also stands. "I'll come with you."

"No, stay here. It's your party."

Victoria is aglow with patio parties, in spite of the mosquitoes. I could just hit the store on the corner, but I've got a wine buzz and the air smells good. I walk down to the Drive. I am a lit female spectator. If anything comes up, I've got a sharp athame in my purse whose teeth have been collecting dust. It's been two months since I quit my job as an Occult Special Investigator. So far, we've been okay. I still make two-thirds of my salary. But my benefits will end soon. I have to make a decision, not tonight, but soon. I am fed up with the tyranny of decision making.

The pubs overflow onto decks that strain to hold the collective intelligence and anxiety of keyed-up graduate students. Everyone is smoking, drinking Keith's, and talking about what program they're in. I pass the co-op bookstore, where a few people still linger over the 'zines. From here, I can discern the rumble of the 135 as it speeds down Twelfth, in its endless pilgrimage up and down Burnaby Mountain.

I step into a convenience store at the corner of Adanac, whose name—Canada spelled backward—has always annoyed me for no good reason. The inside of the store is bright and yellow. Those bastard fluorescent tubes would just love to give me a migraine. I guess I really am the kind of person who carries a dagger but not sunglasses. I stare at the shelves, which mostly disappoint. I fight the desire for tea biscuits. I grab scrubbers, creamer, pop, and mini-eggs, which I thought used to be rationed by the Canadian government but are now apparently always in season. I get toilet paper because there's never enough. I consider buying condoms. Why does this purchase always make me feel like the Whore of Babylon? I decide against it and pick up Sensodyne toothpaste instead. I need to floss more. I wanted to initiate a flossing regime this summer, until Mia pointed out that I was really the only person in the house who didn't floss. I've just never liked the feeling of that razory silk between molars, like a garrote.

As I'm paying for my items, a drunk vampire walks in. At least, I think he's drunk. His expression is weird. Vampires get smarter as their hunger increases, which is why they've survived for so long. It takes a lot of alcohol to faze them, and even then, the spark of unlife remains keen in their eyes. His are glassy. He looks more stoned than drunk. His mouth twitches. Stoned, but peckish.

The earth is also peckish, which I know because I can sense it. I have always heard mountains cough and magma whisper. That second thing actually creeps me out and gives me acid reflux. People like me chat with the universe through materia, which is aware and thirsty. Linus, our DNA technician, once called it a bastard energy, because it makes the universe die faster.

I draw in some earth materia, which makes me want to smoke more than you'd ever believe. I don't throw out anything serious, just a few sparks to let him know that I'm not playing. He stares at me for a few seconds. Then he turns and staggers out the door. I finish paying for my items. The exhausted guy behind the counter has no idea how close he's just come to being someone's nightcap.

I step outside. There's no sign of the vampire. My senses are dull from the wine, so I pause to listen closely. I let the street evaporate. I can still see the buildings, but they're pale before the light of so many night things panting and trying to devour one another. Different flows of materia slip by at astonishing speeds, as if merging onto a metaphysical freeway. The street complains, the telephone poles curse, the water glares, but I sense nothing like a vampire nearby. This relaxes me.

I stop listening and look away, back at the regular world. According to my mother, I was a dangerous little girl. My potential needed to be concealed so that my real father wouldn't find me. Now I'm just a wet firecracker. Everyone knows that you're at your most powerful when you're a kid. I'd missed out on those times. I'd peaked without even knowing it.

Maybe I should visit her. It's late, but I know she'll be up reading. I know I should go back to the party, but for some reason, I'm not ready. I don't quite believe my senses. I walk down to Twelfth. The bus stop is empty. Did I really think that an amped-up vampire would be waiting for the trolley bus? I exhale and walk back up Commercial. I'm in canvas shoes, and my blisters are smarting. Who wouldn't find me sexy tonight?

My phone rings. I figure it's Derrick making a last-minute plea for layered dip, but it's Detective Selena Ward. We've barely talked since I filed my leave papers. I'm suddenly nervous. Is she calling to fire me? Has there been a death in the lab? Sometimes the cadavers in our morgue don't stay dead, and anything can happen when you throw zombies into the mix. I take the call.

"Selena. What's going on?"

She sounds tired, as always. "Look. I know you're off right now. I know you're using this time to think and just get away from all of this. But I need you and Derrick both for a few hours tonight. He'd be working; you'd be consulting."

There are two things I want to say. *I can't because it's Lucian's birthday. I can't because I owe it to my family to make this work.* But Selena has always been unsentimental. I'm left with the realization that seeing a body might be exactly what I need tonight, which is wrong on so many levels.

"Selena—" I sigh. "I don't know. I've been drinking a little, and so has Derrick. Wouldn't it be some kind of union infraction?"

"Lord Nightingale died."

"Excuse me?"

"The ruler of the necromancers, the governor of Trinovantum, is dead. We have an hour to go over everything, and this is a big library."

"He died in a library?"

"Yes. The Bennett Library at Simon Fraser University. You need to get here. Drink coffee, slap yourself—I don't care. I need your help with this. I'm sorry, Tess. With any luck, we'll be out of there before the first hungover students arrive."

She hangs up.

I stare at the phone for a second, as if it's just lied to me. I hardly knew Lord Nightingale. We spoke only a few times, and he'd always unnerved me, although he was attractive and generally polite. I wasn't sure what I felt, knowing that his long life had suddenly been extinguished. Should I bring Lucian? He was Seventh Solium, which was really more of a civil servant gig, as far as I could tell, but he and Lord Nightingale were friends. I couldn't even tell if they liked each other. Men can be so fucking cryptic.

I walk back to the house. I can understand why Selena needs our help, but I can't help but wonder if I'm about to walk into an interrogation. It's never a good thing to have known a murdered prince.

As I reach our driveway, the front door opens, and Derrick appears.

"What did you tell Lucian?"

He manages to look guilty. "I just said I was being called to a scene. I didn't specify. I wasn't sure of the protocol."

"He'll find out in the morning. For now, it's just us."

"Mia's started up a game of Taboo. They'll be good for hours."

We get into the van. Derrick lets it warm up. He tunes the radio to CBC and puts the van in gear. We drive uphill listening to Yo-Yo Ma, whose notes provide a suitable background as we prepare our tool kits. It begins to rain, and Burnaby Mountain is slick, like volcanic glass. We park by the West Mall Complex and walk from there. We pass the Louis Riel residence, where students dream of quarks, Margaret Atwood, and ways to extend their meal plan.

There are no security guards. Our lab uses materia to create a veil, which is really a kind of microwave background noise that keeps people away for a time. Whenever an immortal is killed, we need to act quickly to secure the scene. There are many things that most people aren't meant to see, including the shells of those who defy explanation. SFU seems like too young a campus to hold the body of Lord Nightingale, who grew up in the eleventh century. A necromancer who began life as a woman but died as a man.

How does a thing get immortality? It's a good question. Vampires are bled first. Necromancers are stillborn. Some demons, like reptiles, survive for centuries beneath the painful eye of a dark sun. I can see and touch materia because I share blood with an immortal. My mother got the gene from her grandmother. Then she met my father, who was death. I have a sister who looks like a spinning house on fire. I guess that makes me the normal daughter.

Derrick and I walk through the empty West Mall Building, whose floor is made of red rubber and has a pleasing give to it. The coffee carts are asleep. In the bathrooms, toilets wash themselves at intervals, like somnambulists. We exit the building and head to the Academic Quadrangle, an enclosure walled in granite and glass with a dry fountain. There are stairs everywhere, and in places, the exposed rebar skeleton beneath them. We enter the W. A. C. Bennett Library. There was a time when the thought of an empty library all to myself would have filled me with excitement. Now all the dead terminals and empty chairs seem improper and unnerving. All the chutes are still.

We take the stairs to the fifth floor. The recycled air is hot and tastes of old paper. The floor has just been waxed. When we reach the scene, the first thing I notice is the blood on the photocopiers. The arcs rise and plummet like arterial meter. The machines have old coin slots, now useless appendages, replaced by card readers that charge twelve cents per page. Blood has struck the paper cutter as well as the staplers chained to a nearby table.

Lord Nightingale is on his side. His throat is cut. His blood hasn't completely dried, and air from the vents raises dimples on the large stain.

The absence of our medical examiner is unusual. There are only two people here: my supervisor and a necromancer I haven't seen for nearly two years.

"Deonara Velasco." I incline my head. "Does this—I mean—" I look at Selena uncertainly. "Will she take his place?"

"I already have," Deonara says. "I am Lord Nightingale now."

I look at the body. I saw him alive only twice, once in armor, the second time in a raincoat. He smiled, stepped sideways, and was gone. Now his blood is everywhere, and, like the blood of any immortal, it attracts materia to it. The air is thick, and I have to concentrate to avoid seeing shadows and afterimages everywhere. It will take all night for the water of his life, all nine hundred years of him, to dry like mud and vanish.

"The Soliums are wild with ambition and fear," Deonara says. "Theresa controlled them, but I'm not sure if I can."

I look at Selena. "No weapon?"

She shakes her head. "Just a photocopy card."

I recall Luiz Ordeño's death, which was when I'd last seen Deonara Velasco. He died in a breastplate beneath a two-way painting. The question then had not been, *Who killed him?*, but rather, *What* could *kill him?* Old necromancers, as a rule, were more prone to rage against the dying of the light than to expire passively. I couldn't think of anything, offhand, that could actually kill Lord Nightingale, who for most purposes had already been far from alive.

"All that's important now," Deonara says, "is that we

leave no trace of the shell behind. This act is going to be a magnet for political unrest in both of our cities. We need to stay on top of it."

Selena looks at Derrick. "All right. You're up first. I need you to see if any part of his mind is still broadcasting."

Derrick pulls on a pair of gloves and kneels before the body. He touches the cold hand, slick with blood. He closes his eyes. I feel nothing. The way his mind interprets materia is a mystery to me. I wouldn't want his ability. I already know what people are thinking most of the time. The last thing I need is to hear that neurotic tapestry in surround sound.

He's still for a moment. Then he stands cautiously.

"Was there anything?" Selena asks.

Derrick is expressionless. He blinks, and the veil is gone. He doesn't look at me, only at Selena, and his voice is flat, tired.

"The usual. Pain and fear."

Deonara sighs. "You people had best work quickly. After you're finished, I will purify the site."

We gather samples in silence while the body sucks in everything around us, like a crumbling event horizon. I'm distracted, not because of the situation, but because I know that Derrick is lying.

2

At four thirty a.m. the cleaning crew arrives, and we're allowed to go. I know I should sleep, but the thought of lying down suddenly frightens me. I'd rather be productive than vibrate with anxiety in bed.

"Do you need anything else from me?"

"I don't think so. Thank you."

"I was happy to help."

We neither tell the truth nor lie. Selena and I shake hands and get into our respective vehicles. Deonara vanished hours ago. She just stepped oddly out of a door and was gone. You never know what to expect when dealing with people who can travel through apertures. They're way too good at sneaking up on you.

Derrick takes us through the Tim Hortons drive-through. We drink our coffee in silence until he parks in the driveway. I want to get out of the car, but I have a suspicious mind; I can't help it.

"Wait."

He pauses in the act of removing his seat belt. "What did we forget?"

"Nothing. I need to ask you something."

"Sure."

"What did you see in Lord Nightingale's mind?"

His expression changes. He's not angry or even rueful, since he knows that I can tell when he's lying. He merely looks anxious.

"It was hard to tell for sure."

"Derrick."

"Okay. He was thinking about sex before he died."

"How could you tell?"

"He was aroused."

"Whoa. Was it angel lust?"

"No, that's postmortem wood. This erection was ante-mortem. I guess he was fantasizing about someone."

"Why wouldn't you tell Selena that?"

"It just seemed inconsequential."

"But it's interesting. Maybe it will supply further context."

"The guy's, like, a prince, right? It just seemed a little undignified to say that he had a boner a few seconds before dying."

"I take back my 'whoa' and replace it with 'wow.'"

"Excuse me?"

"Earlier, I said 'whoa,' because what you were describing was kinky. Now I say 'wow,' because I realize that you're still lying to me."

"Tess."

"You're seriously going to play me this way?"

"Please don't try to sound like our kids."

"Derrick, just spit it out. What else did you see?"

He exhales and sinks into the seat. "Okay. I didn't exactly see anything, but I did smell something."

"That's physical evidence—"

"It barely smelled like anything."

"What did it barely smell like?"

"Miles."

"Wow. Whoa. Both. You have to tell Selena."

"What should I tell her? For a second, Lord Nightingale smelled like my boyfriend? That makes no sense."

"Did he smell like Miles, or was he smelling Miles?"

"I don't know. I could just smell one of his shirts. The blue one that makes his arms look really good. Maybe my own mind interfered with the reading. Maybe I only thought I smelled it."

"Maybe they knew each other."

"Miles is a bit prejudiced where necromancers are concerned. Lord Nightingale spent most of his time in Trinovantum. When would they have met?"

"This is why you kept your mouth shut. You're afraid they're connected."

"Of course I'm afraid of that!"

I put a hand on his shoulder. "Look. I'm the queen of murky decisions; we both know that. But I really don't think Miles is cheating on you with a necromancer. Maybe they met by accident once, and he smelled so good that day that—"

"I'll tell her tomorrow morning."

We get out of the van and walk up the driveway. I'm angry, but we both need to chill and this isn't the time for a fight. I can understand lying in the heat of the moment. I've done that. But in the silence of the van's interior, which has always been a confessional cabinet for us, he'd lied again. It's not like him.

Lucian's gone. Mia and Patrick are both asleep. Miles comes into the living room holding a mug of tea. Derrick hugs him, then signs something too quickly for me to translate. Both of them walk down the hallway and into Derrick's room. I sit on the couch and try not to go crazy. The coffee has turned my stomach into a battlefield. I close my eyes and try to be still, but there's too much sugar in my body. I feel warm and slightly damp. I wish for a pool in the living room, and for immortals to stop dying so late at night, and for a peppermint to calm my gut-rot.

I go outside and sit on the patio. The sky is changing color. I start to light a cigarette, but then I hear my mother telling me how it doesn't seem very reasonable to poison yourself slowly, like a torturer. *It's a bit macabre, if you ask me, darling.*

Bleeding Out

I take the athame out of my purse and lay it next to the pack of king-sized silvers. I place my empty coffee cup next to the dagger. These are all vices that have taught me extraordinary things about myself. The athame allows me to work with flows of materia that would normally be too dense and temperamental to manipulate. The blade bears most of the pain, and for a few seconds, I feel like I'm touching solar wind, convection currents, monsoons. That sense of enlargement can be addictive. It's not a high—it's not even pleasant most of the time—but it does remind me that I exist alongside purposeful forces, animals as old as the universe itself. Surely they or something else must know what's supposed to be going on.

I watch the sun come up. I turn on the coffeemaker. I leave out a few fixings for breakfast, along with a Post-it reminding Mia to take her shot. Then I throw on a jacket and walk out the door. I'm overdue for a meeting with my occupational therapist. If I pass out in the middle of the day and his office calls, that doesn't seem like quite the same thing as avoidance, more like a happy accident. Sometimes, the burn of exhaustion is actually what allows me to do my job. It numbs the sounds and colors. I think about how good it will feel to come home, have supper with my family, and crawl into a bed that isn't blood-stained or covered in shrink-wrap.

I walk to Seventh and take the SkyTrain downtown. The brakes on the Expo Line car sound like angry monkeys. The lights flicker only a few times. I get off at

Waterfront Station, which is buzzing. When I walk outside, I can see the harbor and the slick bars that surround it. Harbour Centre gleams on the corner, the perfect fusion of campus, mall, and tourist attraction. You can see the North Shore Mountains from the top of the tower, but the elevator ride will cost you.

I cross the street and walk to our lab, which resembles a government building next to an underground car park. Very few people outside of the occult community know of our existence, but the ones who do are very good at erasing us from view. Like any large city, Vancouver is home to a group of immortals and things whose lives are touched by other worlds. Our lab was designed to investigate crimes within this group, which, for lack of a better word, we call "mystical." Recently, our truce with the vampire nation and the necromancers has started to go south. Luiz Ordeño died to make peace between them, but we've failed to keep it. And now Theresa is gone. I remember the last words that he spoke to me before he vanished into the rain. *If I don't get back, I'll turn into a pumpkin. A very dangerous pumpkin.*

I get past security, all the way to the Trace unit, before I realize that I have no reason for being here. Selena didn't call. I'm not an investigator and I have no business asking questions about an active case. So why did I come here? I'm like an escaped mental patient who's wandered back to her old life in a fugue state. I should leave, but curiosity and lack of professionalism win out. I head to Selena's office.

Her door is closed, and I can hear that she's talking to

someone. There's a trick I can do with the door to shake up
its molecules like ginger ale, which would allow me to hear
a tin-can version of their conversation. I resist. Whenever
I hear my supervisor talking quietly with someone behind
a closed door, I assume I'm being fired. It's a weird prey
instinct that I've had since I was a girl, ears back, always
waiting for the claw to fall. Probably she's just arguing with
Linus about the results of an agarose gel test. I once heard
him saying irritably to her: *Cut the crap; you and I both
know that DNA always migrates toward the camera.*

I lean against the wall. I know that I'm punishing
myself. A normal person on approved leave from their job
would go home and nap with the dog. I think about going
over to Lucian's place. We cannot talk about Theresa, or
at least we should not. We play dangerous Parcheesi with
vampires and necromancers. There are no darkened safe
spaces. We play from our nests and try to get to the heart
of the board. Lucian lives in my city, but he's still an
antagonist.

It's been a few weeks since we did anything but snore
next to each other in bed. We've kissed, but it's all surface
kissing, the kind that leads nowhere specific. He was
grossed out the other day when he saw me peeling a Dr.
Scholl's disc off my heel. I saw his expression change. It
was as if I'd just urinated on his socks or thrown a clump
of bloody hair at him. I get that he's not going to find
corns sexy, but this is real life, and my body does all sorts
of crazy shit.

"Tess."

I turn. It's Ru. He's lived in the lab ever since he crashed here from the world of P'tahl, which is apparently a lot like Jupiter. His gray scales remind me of delicate shingles. His horns are well-groomed. He's wearing jeans and a T-shirt, but no shoes.

"Good morning, Ru."

"Good morning, Tess. I dispensed with vermin today."

I'm not expecting this. "What did you kill them with?" For some reason, this is the only question that enters my mind. Ru's civilization was colonized by another. He's not what I'd traditionally think of as a warrior, but I did once see him spit acid in the face of a horse demon.

"I didn't kill them. I reasoned with them."

"How did you do that?"

"It was difficult, because rat grammar is full of exceptions and everything is in the subjunctive, but I managed to convince them to relocate."

"That's very considerate of you, but you really shouldn't be wandering around the lab at night looking for rats to charm."

"Tess—" He gives me a funny look. I realize that he's trying to save me from embarrassment. "There is not much to do here. I grew up in the middle of a red storm five times larger than Earth. On P'tahl, there are sheets of lightning that stretch fifty miles, devouring the sky. Here it mostly rains."

"I'm sorry, Ru. I wish we had better lightning."

"We must work with what we are given." He glances at Selena's door. "I know who she's talking to."

"Did you see them walk in together?"

"No. But I can hear them now. Lucian Agrado is telling Detective Ward that he has no idea what someone named Theresa was doing in a library."

"Lucian?" I blink. "Is he consulting? If that were the case—"

The door opens before I can finish mumbling. Selena steps out, followed by Lucian, who smiles when he sees me. But my boss isn't smiling.

"Tess. I'm confused. Did we schedule a meeting?"

"No. I—"

Why am I here? It's a simple question, but I have no answer. I'm here because this lab has been my life since I was a teenager. I'm here because I'm a piss-poor homemaker who'd rather be consulting on a homicide. I'm here because I have no idea how to have a mental health vacation, because here is a place whose rules I've internalized, however messed up they might be.

"She is here," Ru says, "to take me for breakfast."

His words are like a small miracle. Selena relaxes. "Sure. Just don't go too far, and put on your people face."

Ru nods. His features ripple, and he becomes a boy, without scales.

"I would like a simian bun," he says.

"You mean cinnamon bun. No problem."

Ru looks at Lucian. "Mr. Agrado, would you like to join us? I believe there will be enough buns."

I don't know what he's playing at, but he's doing a bang-up job of it.

"I'd love to," Lucian says. "If Agent Corday doesn't mind."

"It's fine. The more buns, the merrier."

"That sounds—"

"I know how it sounds. Let's just go. I could use a coffee."

Selena looks at me for a second. I see the wheels turning. I feel like she's about to tell me that I've violated the terms of my leave, or that my information grubbing is transparent. But she simply reaches into her wallet and gives Ru a toonie.

"Bring me back something glazed," she says. "No walnuts."

Ru never leaves the lab unescorted. He's strong and resourceful, but this isn't his world. It's not safe for him here. It's not really safe for anyone here. He walks between us while we head down Robson. The hot dog carts have lines, and the clouds are indecisive, which means that everyone's in T-shirts and Birkenstocks.

"Can we visit the musical archive?" Ru asks.

"Do you mean HMV?"

"Yes. The place with the listening booths."

I look at Lucian. He shrugs. The store is loud and crowded, but I doubt that anything will happen.

"Fine," I say. "They probably have a fully functioning restaurant by now. We can hang out there for a bit; then we'll grab a coffee and take you back."

We walk in. They're playing top-forty music at earsplitting levels. Ru heads straight for the escalator, which is his favorite thing. I remember when this building used to be the library, before it was relocated farther downtown. It became a Virgin Megastore (which sounds like an emporium for sacrificial must-haves). Now it's owned by another company, but the layout is the same. It's weird to think that this place used to be full of books. Now it's full of bored teenagers and confused adults. I hear a familiar chorus. *So coast in slow over Reno.* Lucian puts his arm around me. I remember when we danced to this song, just before we were nearly killed by an Iblis. Simpler times.

Ru heads for the box sets in the basement. It's freezing down here, and there are less people. I can't tell the customers from the employees. Sometimes people emerge from a long corridor in the back, but everyone's wearing the same clothes; everyone's carrying merchandise. They might be coming from anywhere. Lucian thumbs his way through the foreign film section. I look at the posters, which are mostly of superheroes and women in microshorts. None of them seem appropriate for Ru. Now, if they had a poster of Jupiter, we'd be in business.

I'm just about to ask one of the non-salespeople if they have an astronomy section when everything gets quiet. My senses are awake. Something's different. I go in search of Lucian, but he's wandered off somewhere. I send him a text: *meet me out front.* It could just be a few stoner vampires craving music, but that's a best-case scenario. I walk around the basement in circles. Ru's not here. I take the escalator to the mezzanine floor, and find him browsing through techno albums.

"Tess." He waves. "They have the new DJ Tiësto."

"We're leaving," I say quietly.

"Oh. Because of the vampires?"

I always forget what a good nose he has. "How many are there?"

"Four. They smell different, though. Strange."

"Strange good?"

"English is not my first language, but is strange ever good?"

"No." I sigh. "Okay. Lucian's meeting us out front. With any luck, they won't even notice us leave."

We take the stairs to the ground floor. I see the vampires. One of them looks right at me, and it's like a kick to the stomach. He's the one I saw in the convenience store last night. His eyes are still glassy. He smiles.

I grab Ru's arm.

"Follow me. As soon as we get outside, they'll scatter."

"Your words do not match your feelings."

"Excuse me?" I steer him toward the entrance.

"Your breathing has quickened. Your heart rate is elevated. Why should vampires make you so nervous? Your city is full of them."

We exit the store, and sunlight breaks over my face. Lucian's there. He gives me a funny look.

"In a hurry?"

I try to look like I'm not freaking out. "Nah. I just couldn't stand the air-conditioning in there anymore. Do you mind if we go?"

"It's not up to me. The afternoon belongs to Ru."

He stares at both of us impassively. I want to use sign language to say, *Not a word about the vampires*, but Lucian can speak ASL. All I can do is take a breath and trust in fate not to screw me over.

"I'm hungry," Ru says. "Let's go."

He takes my right hand. Lucian takes my left. How do creatures like us find each other? After years of listening to the universe in tremors and lit wicks, I still don't know what's driving it all, what's driving us. Ru's hand is small and cold in mine. I try to imagine him running from chain lightning, or toward it, playing chicken.

We get our coffee and doughnuts. As Lucian pays, it occurs to me that he's said absolutely nothing about Theresa's death. I imagine that's what he and Selena were talking about. Why else would he have been in her office? I'm starting to get twitchy around him. Lucian and the late Lord Nightingale were close in some way that only necromancers understand. It seems only fair that we should talk about it over tequila shots, or something along those lines. But he isn't saying a word.

We grab coffee and take Ru back to the lab. He stays quiet about the vampires that we saw in HMV. There was something off about them, and not just because they were tempting fate by day-walking. I make a note to ask Patrick about it when I get home, although chances are he'll be burning the midnight heme, or whatever vampires call working late. Lucian and I walk through multiple security checks without speaking. He surrenders his visitor pass at the front desk. We walk outside, and the sun is so bright it's almost cruel. I shield my eyes for a second. The glass and steel of downtown Vancouver burns with trapped heat. I feel like if I laid my cheek against any surface, it would sizzle. That might actually look pretty neat.

"Where are you off to?" Lucian asks.

"I was going to go home. I need to buy groceries first, though. There's nothing in the fridge except vermouth and Babybel cheese."

"You could come over to my place."

"I could. Do you want to watch a movie?"

He shrugs. This could mean either sex or *Star Trek*. I suppose I at least have a fifty-fifty chance of relieving some tension. As long as we don't have to watch the episode where Captain Picard gets tortured by Cardassians. We walk to Yaletown. By the time we reach his apartment, I've sweat through my blouse and my feet hurt, which is my own fault for wearing these stupid sandals that have proved impossible to break in. I watch Lucian as he fishes in his pockets for the key. His hands are lovely. His ass looks great in a pair of broken-down cargo jeans. I wonder why we're still together, which is a favorite neurotic record that I like to play. The greatest hits of my imposter syndrome. Lucian could be with anyone, but for some reason, he chose me. I've never been able to figure out why. Before we met, he was hooking up with Sabine Delacroix, a vampire who looked like Jessica Rabbit. If that was his type, then why would he suddenly switch to dating someone like me?

The living room is cool, thanks to the central air. I'm about to sit down on the couch when I remember how soaked my shirt is. I'm not willing to smell myself, but I know that it can't be good.

"I'm going to have a shower," I say.

"Okay. I think there's still some of your conditioner left."

"Good. I'm not using your two-in-one."

"There's nothing wrong with it."

"Lucian, it's abnormal for a product to be both shampoo and bodywash. I'll stick to what I know."

"Fine." He kisses me on the cheek. "I'll prepare something to eat."

I walk upstairs. His bathroom is bright and spotless. I strip off my clothes and step into the shower. The water raises goose bumps on my skin. I remember the first time I showered after visiting an occult crime scene. I could still smell the burning ammonia of goblin blood, which had gotten into my hair. I open my eyes and look down at the clear water swirling around my feet. No more blood. I guess this is what it means to take a vacation from the field: showers that don't always end in having to disinfect the tub. I work some conditioner into my angry hair, which now resembles a knotted bedsheet. It weirds me out that I can't find a single trace of Lucian in the shower: no skin cells, no stray follicles, nothing. How does he always manage to clean up after himself so well? That's never something I've been adept at.

Once my hair has reached the point where I might actually be able to run a comb through it, I turn off the water and step onto the cold tiles. He's laid out a fresh towel for me, which smells of his fabric softener. I dry myself off and go to his room, where I always keep a contingency outfit. Not my sexiest ensemble ever, but at least it's clean. As I'm pulling on the shirt, I notice that he's left his smartphone on the bed. The red light is blinking. I pick it up gingerly. There's a new text message.

This must be a test. The universe is testing me to see if I'm a good human being. I should respect his privacy. But, at heart, I'm an investigator. I need to find things out, even when they're bad. Especially when they're bad.

"No," I murmur. "Just take the phone to him."

It could be the new Lord Nightingale. I doubt she'd say anything pertinent about this case via text message, but one never knows. Maybe it's an ex. Oh, God, maybe he's sleeping with the new Lord Nightingale, just like he slept with the old one. Sure, it was only one time, but old habits die hard.

"Be a better person," I tell myself. "You can do it."

I pick up the phone and click on the new message. Clearly, I wasn't chosen for this profession because I'm trusting. In the soul of every investigator, there's an only child who wants to know every last detail, even if it hurts.

The message is from an unknown number. It says:

Night, bro.

I put down the phone. I suddenly feel cold. Lucian did have a brother, Lorenzo, but he died. The text must be some kind of joke. I mark the message as unread and go downstairs.

3

I have an appointment with my occupational ther-apist this morning. In exchange for my paid leave of absence, I had to sign a contract saying that I would see Dr. Lori Hinzelmann more often. I'm not sure what these sessions are supposed to accomplish, other than reminding me at regular intervals how crazy I am. I drew the line a year ago when he asked me to sketch the anger I felt toward all the demons who had tried to kill me in the past. Now he mostly just grills me about my personal life, which never fails to provide sundry material for discourse. It's a bit unreal having a four-foot-tall kobold ask you about your erotic dreams, but then again, most things in my line of work lean toward the bizarre. At least his office has an espresso machine.

The SkyTrain flies me over Commercial Drive. I look through the glass as the tops of trees and buildings whip by. Vancouver exports most of its smog to the Fraser Valley, so the air is clear. I see the shadows of mountains and unlaced clouds. People around me doze, do crosswords, and listen to music that their earbuds can't contain. The various Auto-Tuned voices and synthetic beats murmur in the air. There's a trick with aerobic materia that would let me block out the sound, but my mother taught me never to waste power on the things that annoy us. I content myself with looking at the blue fabric of the empty seat across from mine, which resembles movie theater carpet.

I was still a teenager when I was selected by the CORE to become an Occult Special Investigator. They like to headhunt people with any capacity for manipulating natural forces, and when your father's a pureblood demon, you tend to have that in spades. At the time, I didn't actually know that my mother had power as well. I thought I'd inherited it solely from my father's side of the family. There's still a lot I don't know about my mother. I look out the window again, as if expecting to see her flying alongside the SkyTrain, waving at me. But all I see are the buildings on Main Street and, between them, patches of blue space.

As far as I know, I'm the only person on this train who can see the energies that make life possible, the torsions and cosmic flares that drive everything. I see the blood and nerves of the universe, but its narrative stays hidden.

Sometimes it's all too much. I want to be normal and nearsighted. I want to live in a world where demons are just something Hollywood uses to sell movie tickets.

I get off at Burrard Station and walk to the CORE building, which houses multiple offices in addition to the occult Forensics unit. The foyer is all slick marble and track lighting, but within the stone and under the air, power curls hot and sweet like dragon breath. I pass through the necessary checkpoints and step into the elevator, along with several other people. A few of them I've seen before, but don't know by name. We smile politely. We keep silent, which is the first rule. The less we know about each other's domains, the better.

I step off the elevator and into an air-conditioned waiting room. I check in at the desk and then take a seat. People just like me are reading old issues of *Chatelaine* or cycling through various menus on their smartphones. I guess it should be a comfort to know that I'm not the only person in my line of work who needs therapy. It should be, but I still feel like a lone freak. Derrick is a telepath and he doesn't feel the need to unburden himself to a goblin therapist.

When it's my turn, I walk down the hallway that leads to Dr. Hinzelmann's office. He looks up and smiles. His eyes are the color of maple syrup, with slit pupils. I sit on the couch, which I've come to think of as the divan of discontent, since contact with its cushions is usually a prelude to feeling bad for the next forty minutes.

Dr. Hinzelmann opens a green folder. My green folder. All of his folders are color-coded, but I've never managed to crack his chromatic code. He glances down at it for a few seconds, then looks at me.

"How are you?"

This question is a trap waiting to be sprung. I've tried every conceivable answer, but none of them works. Inevitably, he ends up finding some crack in my resolve. There's no such thing as feeling fine in this office. Fine means that you could be better. Fine means that you should consider letting go of your anger, and I can't explain to him that my anger is what keeps me warm.

"Fine," I say.

"Relaxed?"

"Sure. I've been sleeping better."

"That's good to hear."

Lying to him is useless. He sees through every confabulation as if it were made of tissue paper. His eyes scan me. If this were a psychic attack, I could raise a defense, but there's no adequate ward against a PhD from Johns Hopkins. I feel like he knows my mind, like he's seen hundreds of minds like mine, obscure and boring. My childish fracture points are as easily divinable to him as a connect-the-dots picture in a child's coloring book. He smiles. He always smiles before he strikes.

"Would you like some coffee?"

"I already had some. Thanks, though."

"Really, I just like turning the dials on the machine."

I almost say, *That makes sense*, but it feels racist. Being a goblin doesn't make him mechanically inclined. Or does it? I should have paid more attention in my demon anthropology classes. I should pay more attention in general. I can't remember where Mia said she'd be today, even though she told me twice. I can't remember whose turn it is to make supper. I could ask Derrick to bring home Sky Dragon, but lately he's had this weird issue with the chow mein. Something about the noodles being too fat, or maybe not fat enough.

"Tess?"

Dr. Hinzelmann is staring at me good-naturedly. I want to lunge over his desk and grab the green file, which contains all of my nightmares, everything that's ever made me ashamed, and probably a few sexual peccadilloes. Instead, I put both hands in my pockets and smile.

"Sorry. I spaced."

"Where were you?"

Don't mention Lucian or the text message. Don't mention that you feel gross and unattractive. Don't mention the time you saw him buying pants in the junior department at Sears. Goblins have to shop somewhere, right? And those Nevada cargos were pretty sharp. Almost kicky.

"I don't know." I lean back. "Sometimes I never know."

"The goal of these sessions—one of the goals, at any rate—is to determine whether this break that you've requested should be temporary, or permanent. Do you feel like you've made any headway in answering this question for yourself?"

"Not really."

"Why do you think you needed time off?"

"Well, a Kentauros demon tried to kill me. I mean, not just me. He tried to kill a bunch of people, but I was pretty high on his list. Then I met my biological sister, who, as it turns out, is an enraged waterspout who killed Ru's brother. It was by accident, but still—it freaked me out. My family is messed up."

"All families are psychotic, Tess."

"Oh, really? Is your sister a demonic intelligence who sends you nightmares because she has a daddy complex?"

"No. But we're not talking about my sister. Tell me about Arcadia."

"First tell me something about your family."

"That's not how it works, Tess."

I cross my arms. "Fine. I promise to lay out all my tangled emotions for you, like some kind of soiled, neurotic duvet. Just tell me one thing about this sister of yours."

He hesitates. His expression changes. I can tell that, like me, he's actually troubled by his own flesh and blood. Then he sighs. His felid pupils float sadly in their liquor of gold. His mouth hardens.

"My sister is an angry person," he says. "When we were children, she used to find animals and torture them. She liked it when they screamed. She never killed anything, but I could tell that she wanted to. I was always frightened that she'd have children, but she never did. Now she works in an office. We see each other on holidays. We're friends on Facebook. But whenever I hear her laugh, all I can think of is how happy it used to make her to pull the whiskers off cats."

I stare at him. Dr. Hinzelmann has never said anything even remotely like this before. Somehow, I imagined his family to be normal, or at least as normal as a goblin family could be. Maybe he's lying just to get a rise out of me. I don't think so, though. Animal cruelty doesn't seem like the type of casual lie you'd use to assuage your patient that she isn't the only one in the world with problems.

"I'm sorry," I say.

He shrugs. "Family. There's nothing you can do about them."

"I guess not."

"So tell me about Arcadia."

"I don't really know anything about her, except that she's one of the Ferid, and she could take me apart just by looking at me."

"But she didn't."

"No. She restrained herself."

He glances at his notes. "She told you something about your father. What was that, exactly?"

"She told me that he was a bastard, which I already knew."

"That's not what you said earlier."

It's not fair that he gets to consult notes every time we talk. Maybe I should start taking notes. I tried to use the journal function on my phone once, but I only ended up writing bad poetry.

"She told me"—I sigh—"that my mother was hiding something. She's always maintained that my father assaulted her. But Arcadia said that isn't what happened at all. I'm more inclined to believe my mother than a crazy demon I only just met."

"But you suspect that she may be right."

"I didn't say that."

He looks at me flatly. "No. You didn't. But your comportment suggests that you didn't completely discount what Arcadia had to say."

"My comportment? What is this, an eighteenth-century masquerade?"

"Tess."

"Fine. She could be right. My mother's lied about all kinds of things before. But it just seems—I don't know— why would she lie about *that*?"

"When did she first tell you that she had been assaulted?"

"Years ago. I was fifteen. No. Sixteen."

"Tell me about that conversation."

"I'd really rather not."

"Okay. Just give me a few details. Where did it happen?"

I feel myself grow slightly cold. "In the car."

"Where were you driving?"

"She was going to work. We were arguing about something. She pulled over to the side of the road. I could tell that she was upset, but I was being a bitch. I didn't want to apologize. I just wanted to get my own way."

"Do you remember what you were arguing about?"

"A guy that I liked. Terry. He was an asshole, and my mom was trying to warn me, but I wouldn't listen."

"How did she warn you?"

The cold spreads from my stomach to my arms, then to my fingers. I can't look at her. I stare out the window as rain gathers on the glass. Her fingers are pale on the steering wheel. She sighs.

He's not good for you, she says. *He has a look. I've seen it before.*

"What do you think she meant by that?"

You think you know everything, I tell her. *But we're not the same. Just because you slept with some stranger and had me doesn't mean I'm going to do the same thing. I'm not that stupid. I know what I'm doing.*

Back then, she says, *I thought I knew everything, too.*

"I asked her who he was. I asked her how it happened."

"And what did she say?"

I look into his golden eyes. "She said he grabbed her on the street. Nobody else was there. She fought back, but he was too strong. He left her in a parking lot. That's where Kevin found her, bleeding, semiconscious. He took her to the hospital. Nine months later, I was born."

"She told you that exactly?"

"She told me everything but which parking lot it was. I've always wanted to know. It's perverse, but still—I can't help being curious."

"Why do you think your mother would construct such an elaborate lie about something so terrible?"

"I don't think she would. That's why I'm confused."

"So Arcadia must be lying."

"She said she was giving me nightmares so that I'd hate my father as much as she did. But the nightmares didn't start until after my mother told me. So I already hated him. It seems like overkill."

"Have you and your mother talked about this recently?"

"It's not exactly her favorite topic."

"Did you ever talk about it after that initial conversation?"

"Once or twice, maybe. But there isn't much to analyze. She always said I was the miracle that came out of it. She'd rather focus on the good."

"Tess—" His voice changes. He glances down at my file. "There's something I have to tell you. I don't know if it's necessarily the right thing to do, but I feel like you deserve to know this."

"Is my medical insurance about to run out? Derrick's is pretty good, but it won't cover everything. If Mia needs braces—"

"It's not that."

"What is it, then?"

He hesitates again. I don't think I've ever seen Dr. Hinzelmann hesitate over anything before today, and now he's done it twice in as many minutes. The cold spreads to all of my extremities. I want to close my eyes, but I don't. I look at him.

"The CORE has access to your medical records, as well as your mother's," he says. "I'm sure you know that already. I can't tell you what's in your mother's file, but I can tell you what's not in it. There is no police report and no hospital report that she underwent any kind of examination. No sexual assault kit was performed. If she really did visit a hospital after this happened, there would be a record."

I'm not sure how to absorb this. For a few seconds, I try to speak, but nothing comes out. Finally, I swallow and summon my voice.

"Why are you telling me this?"

"Because—"

"Right, because you think I deserve to know. Fine, that's noble of you. But why are you telling me this now, after we've been talking for two years? Why are you telling me this today?"

Dr. Hinzelmann lowers his chair and walks over to me. Standing, he barely comes up to my knees. His look is professional, but beneath it, there's a faint trace of what might actually be remorse.

"I'm telling you this," he says, "because it's something you could have easily discovered on your own, years ago. But I don't think you ever wanted to. I'm telling you because, until you resolve your family issues, you'll never be able to commit yourself fully to this job. You can never truly know yourself until you know where you've come from, and someone is lying to you about that. You need to find the truth."

I stand up. "You're wrong. Unless I'd had access to my mother's file, I never would have learned this."

"You could have used any number of forensic data-bases to see if your mother had ever filed an assault report. Maybe it wouldn't have been the kindest or most ethical thing to do, but it's always been within your power. Yet you didn't."

I feel like I might be sick. Bile rises in my throat.

"I have to go," I say.

"I'm sorry, Tess. I didn't mean to upset you."

"Fuck you, Lori."

I walk out of his office, straight to the elevator. I'm alone. When the doors close, I slam my hand against the steel walls. I strike them again and again, until my knuckles start to bleed. Then, shaking, I press the ground-floor button. I stare at myself in the stainless steel panel. I'm a strange daguerreotype about to come undone. The elevator is halfway to the ground floor when I realize that talking to anyone in my family about this would be a mistake. They're what are blocking me, deflecting all of my shots like the goalie whose crease remains sacrosanct. Going through them isn't going to work anymore. I can only go around them.

I reach out and press the button for the subbasement. There's a tiny shock as the biometrics scan me. I figure that Selena doesn't have the time or the inclination to limit my security in the elevator's firmware. I'm right. The elevator descends. I'm sure there are levels even deeper than this one. The CORE building is like a desert phreatophyte with roots that go on for miles below. My clearance stops at the subbasement, but Selena has access to deeper floors. I don't think I want to visit them.

The doors open. I walk down the corridor that leads to the office of our data keeper, Esther. She looks up from her oval desk when I walk in. A scattering of pictures leaps across the surface of her black lenses. For a second, I think I see Derrick's face. But it's gone as quickly as it appeared. Behind Esther, the wall is a hive of data keys, each one a blinking or solid light. I'm not sure what the distinction is, but I know that every one of us is up there, kept and held.

"Tess. How can I help you?"

I opt for the truth. "I need to see if my mother checked into a CORE clinic a year before I was born."

The dim light and the size of her glasses make it nearly impossible to judge her expression. I can't even imagine what she's thinking. She's silent for a beat; then I hear the sounds of her fingers tapping beneath the desk.

"I'm searching LOOM for a record. Our clinics keep detailed files on every type of examination, no matter how minor." She looks down for a moment. "There's something here from 1984."

"What was she examined for?"

Esther looks up. I see my mother's face in her eyes. Then the image is replaced by screen void of characters, save for a blinking ASCII character.

"Why do you need to know this?"

It's a good question. How do I know that Dr. Hinzelmann isn't just messing with me so that he can log in therapy hours? What do I think this single document is going to tell me about my mother, about myself?

"Because it's haunting me," I say.

Esther considers this for a second. Then she says: "Your mother checked into clinic twenty-one B with broken ribs and a concussion. The cause of the injuries was listed as a vehicular accident."

My eyes widen. "That's not possible."

"The examination was carried out by a nurse. Evelyn Stark. I believe she's head nurse now, but at the time, she was still in training."

"A car crash," I say.

"That's what the examination record indicates."

"Was it a hit-and-run?"

"It just says vehicular accident. If you like, I can search the RCMP database to see if an accident was reported that night."

I exhale. "Sure. How long will that take?"

"Twelve seconds."

We're silent as we wait. I look at the blinking data keys. What if I just pulled mine out and ran? What would they do to me? The truth is that I don't know. Most of the time, I feel like the CORE is simply playing with me. I wonder what it would be like to be Esther, holding all of the data.

"There's nothing," she says. "If she was involved in a car accident, nobody reported it. Not even after the fact."

"This isn't right. Why would she falsify a report?"

"How do you know the report is false?"

"Because—" I shake my head. "I guess I don't. But she told me that she went to a hospital. She told my step-dad, Kevin, that she was assaulted."

"Assaulted by whom?"

"I don't know anymore. I have to go. Sorry to be so cryptic, Esther. Thanks for your help."

"You're welcome." Her lenses blink. I see myself. My face is so pale, I can't tell if I'm dead or alive. Then the glasses go dark again. The cursor reappears.

I walk out of her office and take the elevator to the ground floor. I could go to the clinic tonight, but I don't know if Evelyn is working. I don't even know what I'm going to ask her. I don't know if my mother lied to the nurse who examined her, or if her injuries really were consistent with vehicular trauma. Right now, I don't have the energy to take a bus to Kitsilano, where clinic 21B is located. After the travesty of my therapy session, and now this, all I want to do is hurl myself into a *Gilmore Girls* coma.

I take the SkyTrain home to Commercial Drive. When

I walk in, I smell chicken curry. I put down my purse and walk into the kitchen. To my surprise, it's not Derrick cooking, but Mia. She's even wearing an apron.

"Hey. That smells incredible."

"Thanks. It's my first venture into curries, so please, lower your standards. Derrick and Miles should be here in half an hour."

"Patrick?"

"Out somewhere. Which is annoying, because he was supposed to buy raisins, but instead he bailed and I had to walk down to Norman's Fruit Salad to get some."

"How can I help?"

"Don't worry. I've got this."

"Yeah." I smile. "I can see that."

"How was non-work?"

"It was—weird."

"How's *Lucian*?"

"Why are you saying his name that way?"

"Because you obviously stayed at his place last night."

"He's fine. We're fine."

She turns to look at me. She's holding a plastic spoon. Her hair is tied back, and it looks like she could conquer the world. My kid. Only, she's not my kid anymore, if she ever was. In a few months she'll be in college. I don't want her to recede. I want her to stay just like this, funny, angelic, armed.

"You guys are amazing," she says.

"Are we?"

"You're such a power couple. I love you both."

"We love you back."

"Sit down, Tess. Relax. Prepare yourself for a taste experience. It may end in ordering pizza, but at this point, it's still promising."

"That's my favorite time," I murmur, taking a seat.

4

When I was a little girl, I had a stuffed pig that I used to pretend was my sister. I named her Judy. Once, my mother asked me what Judy's voice sounded like, and I replied with confidence: "Medium-high." To this day, I don't know what I meant, but I do know that I took Judy everywhere. She and I would have long conversations about whatever I held dear at the moment. As an only child, I had no idea of what siblings actually discussed in the intimacy of their shared bedrooms. Whenever I was invited to a sleepover, I would ask my friends questions about their brothers and sisters. What did they look like? What games did they play? What was the pitch of their voices? I must have been annoying, but at the time,

I felt like a journalist. If I had a real sister, would she be just like me, or would she be my antipode?

As it turns out, I do have a sister, but I hope that we're nothing alike.

I hear keys in the front door. A moment later, Derrick and Miles enter the kitchen, with Lucian in tow. He sees me and smiles sheepishly.

"We ran into each other at the grocery store," he says.

Derrick is already cramming things into the fridge. "He was about to buy frozen Thai food. I couldn't just leave him like that."

"Makes sense," I say. "Friends don't let friends eat frozen entrées."

He sits down next to me. "I'm stoked about curry."

"I'll tell you what I just told Tess," Mia says. "Don't get your stokes up. This could suck."

"Fine. Stoke disengaged. I have no feelings about curry."

"That's better."

Derrick opens a bottle of wine. By the time dinner is ready, we've moved on to a second bottle, and I'm starting to feel a bit more philosophical about my day. Sure, it's possible that the story of my birth is an enormous lie. Why not just add it to the pile? Everybody lies. If we didn't, talking would be unbearable.

Mia serves the curry, which is stellar. We're about halfway through the second bottle of Shiraz when I hear the front door. Patrick walks into the kitchen.

"You're home early," Mia says.

"Yeah." He has a weird smile. "Tonight's business didn't take as long as I thought it would. Dinner smells awesome."

"There's a plate for you in the fridge."

Patrick grabs his portion and sits down across from me. His eyes are strangely cloudy, and I can smell something familiar on his skin. It's almost—

"Have you been drinking?" I ask.

"No. I drove here."

"I wasn't talking about alcohol."

"Tess—" Mia begins.

I shake my head. "You're completely juiced."

"I am not."

"Patrick, your eyes are practically red."

Anger flashes across his face. "What does it matter?"

"It matters because I can smell the blood on you."

He stands up. "*God.* Why do you always have to stigmatize me? I drink blood. I'm a fucking vampire, Tess."

"Watch your language."

"Don't talk to me like I'm some kind of monster. I can smell the materia on you, but I don't make you feel like shit about it. Why are you always getting on my case about something that I can't control?"

"I'm only asking you to show a little restraint. When you come to dinner all blissed out on heme, it's like—"

"What? Like I really am a demon who drinks blood to survive? Or would you prefer that I keep that part of my life a secret?"

"I'm not saying that—"

"Both of you knock it off," Mia snaps. "Patrick, sit down. I cooked, and we're going to have a normal, insult-free dinner."

Patrick looks at me expectantly.

I sigh. "I'm sorry. You're right. I'm being a hypocrite."

"And a necrophobe."

"I'm dating a necromancer. How can I be necrophobic?"

Lucian glares at me. "That's like saying you can't possibly be racist because you're dating a person of color."

"Sorry. Please don't ask me to read Gloria Anzaldúa again."

"I swear," Mia says, "if you don't shut up and eat this food that I lovingly prepared, I will kill each and every one of you."

I reach across the table and take Patrick's hand. "Darling. I'm sorry. There's no part of you that I don't love."

"I could do without his morning farts," Mia says beneath her breath.

I kiss his fingers. "I even love those."

Miles makes a face. "Can we change the subject?"

"Absolutely." Derrick refills his glass. "Any suggestions?"

Lucian grins. "How about first loves?"

I stare at him. "You really want to go there?"

"I prefer discoursing on love to talking about vampire farts."

"Fine. You first, then. Who was your first love?"

"You."

"Oh, fuck off."

"Language," Patrick says. But he's smiling.

I shake my head. "Dude, you've been alive since before the Spanish Civil War. You've had way more experiences than I have. You expect me to believe that you never fell in love with a single person before we met?"

He shrugs. "I've loved people. I've been attracted to people. But it was all shadowboxing. You're my main event. You're what matters."

I don't know what to say. Everyone's staring at us. I'm afraid I might throw up or start crying. Possibly both.

"I'm your boxing metaphor?" I whisper.

"You're my beloved."

He kisses me. It's the kind of kiss that makes you wish you weren't in a room surrounded by your family. I blush.

"Great," Derrick says. "Someone's supposed to top that?"

I grin. "Go ahead. I know exactly what you're going to say."

"Oh, do you?"

"I think I do."

He sighs. "Man. You do know me well."

"So who was he?" Miles asks.

"It's embarrassing."

"Wait until you hear mine."

"Okay. His name was Stuart. He was my camp counselor."

"Oh wow," Mia says. "Finally, something dirty."

"Nothing happened! We ate marshmallows and played 'The John B. Sails' on the ukulele. All I could do was admire him from afar."

"Aw." Miles kisses him on the cheek. "That's creepy."

"Please don't sully my campfire romance."

"You're right. It's sweet."

"So."

"So what?"

Derrick gives him a look. "I told you mine."

"*Ah—*" Mia leans in closer. "Now I'm curious. Who was it that captured the heart of Miles Sedgwick?"

"It's a bit tragic."

"More tragic than Derrick stalking his camp counselor?"

He glares at Mia. "I was eleven. I wasn't stalking anyone."

"Hush," I say. "Continue, Miles."

Miles looks momentarily uncomfortable beneath the weight of our eyes. Then he shrugs and fiddles with his hearing aid. "His name was Phil. He was blond. We defiled his tree house."

"Whoa." Derrick high-fives him. "Way to go."

"When his family moved, he left me all of his comics. Sweet boy."

I look at Mia. "You've been awfully vocal about getting people to tell their stories. What about you?"

"What about me, Tess?"

"You know I hate it when you use my name like that."

"Like what?"

"Just answer the question."

"I—" She looks down. "It's stupid."

"I wanted to get into Stuart's kayak," Derrick says. "There's no judgment at this table. Love is love."

She looks at Patrick for a second. He seems on the verge of saying something, but keeps his mouth shut.

"It was just some guy in the fourth grade," she says. "I don't even remember his name. He talked to me a few times—whatever. I haven't lived long enough to have the kind of stories that you all have."

I feel like she's lying, but I don't know why. Embarrassment? Remorse? Maybe she hasn't fallen in love with anyone yet. It was stupid of me to press her. The last thing a teenage girl wants is to discuss romance in front of her family.

"You're still figuring things out," I say. "You've got all the time in the world. And, Patrick? What about you? I know you've been busy magnating it for the past few years, but before that—"

I almost say *when you were human*. Man, I'm really batting a thousand in the insensitivity department tonight. I bite off the words and simply smile. I hope it resembles the smile of an attentive parent rather than that of a bitchy misanthrope who may be the smallest bit necrophobic.

"Patty Smalls," he says. "We met in kindergarten. She had freckles, and she gave me a scratch-and-sniff valentine. It's one of the few things I remember from before I was turned."

Mia grins. "Hot."

"Shut up."

"All right, Diotima," Derrick says. "You're the only one left. Spill. Who was your first love? And don't say me, even though we both know that you once had a wicked crush."

"Don't flatter yourself, pretty boy."

Everyone's looking at me. Everyone's smiling. The cold, ineluctable truth is that I don't know if I've ever been in love. I've had feelings. I've lusted, coveted, longed for what I couldn't have. I've been with people in the dark. Probably too many. But if love is the astonishing nude trust in Lucian's eyes, then—

Then?

I love you all, I want to say. *I love you so much it kills me. I'd set fire to myself to keep any one of you from harm. That's what I'm certain of.*

"My math teacher," I say weakly. "He looked cute in flannel."

Mia gives me an odd look.

Now we've both told a lie.

Bleeding Out

* * *

I wake up to an empty house. It's the wine's fault.
I give myself a few more minutes of lucid-dream time,
then drag myself out of bed. Lucian's shirt hangs from
the doorknob. It's unlike him to leave clothing here. He
may love me, but he's pretty cagey about his things. I put
it on, and find that it fits surprisingly well as an overshirt,
in addition to smelling nice. My jeans are starting to smell
like bad cookies, but I know I can wring one more day
out of them. I argue with my hair for a while, finally
combing it into a weird bun that makes me want to punch
the mirror, but at least I can go outside. I check my phone
as I'm going downstairs. There's a text from Derrick invit-
ing me to lunch at Milestones, which he knows I can't
resist due to the circumference of their Bellinis. There's
nothing from work, which disappoints me, although I'm
not completely sure why. Any day without an autopsy
should be good, right?

I have an hour before I have to meet Derrick. I grab
the 20 bus, which sparks and rocks on its cables until we
reach the west end. I walk down Granville, which smells
like pizza and pot. I don't really know where I'm going.
The gathering clouds threaten rain, but don't quite deliver.
I find myself standing in front of a familiar building: a
club, formerly Moonbase, which has been renamed Blood
Drive. Vampires think they're so damn clever. This was
where I first met Lucian. At the time, he was working for

Sabine Delacroix, who ran the club when she wasn't busy killing people.

I stare at the door, which has been painted black. This is where everything started. I remember Lucian offering me a beer, and Sabine placing her hand on my leg, a hand that would later choke me. I remember seeing Patrick, asleep, hooked up to machines that scrutinized the progress of his virus. It wasn't that long ago, but I feel like whoever I was then is gone. I blinked and missed her.

The door opens as I'm standing there. A familiar vampire walks out, wearing shades. It's the same bouncer who talked to me years ago.

"Hey." I smile. "Remember when you smelled me?"

"Of course. How could my nose forget?"

"You haven't changed."

"I'm dead."

"Well, it suits you."

"Thanks. Is there something you wanted?"

"I was just in the neighborhood. I like the new name."

"It's sardonic."

"Yeah. I got that."

His mouth twitches. It's almost a grin. "How's Lucian?"

"Fine."

"We all miss him."

"I'll bet." I decide to try something. "Hey. Here's a question. Have you noticed any seriously tweaked vampires in this neighborhood?"

"Tweaked on what?"

"I don't know. It looks kind of like bloodlust, only glassier. Somewhere between hungry and stoned."

He's silent. I wonder if he's considering whether or not he should say anything. I try to look slightly vapid, like a tourist asking where BC Place is.

"Vampires don't get stoned," he says finally. "THC barely affects us. We can get drunk, if the alcohol is strong enough."

"He'd have smelled, if that were the case."

"Where did you see this vampire?"

"Once in my neighborhood, and once closer to downtown."

He lights a cigarette. "Ask the Magnate. Aren't you two close?"

"Not lately."

"Ask Modred, then. He knows more anyhow. With all due respect to the Magnate, of course."

"That's actually a good idea."

"Well. I have my moments."

I turn to leave. Then I stop.

"What's your name?"

"None of your business."

I laugh. "Fair enough."

He stubs out the cigarette and walks back inside, shutting the door behind him. In my mind, I think I'm going to call him Ruben from now on. I could walk to the vampire community center to speak with Modred, but it seems pointless. I can't ask the right hand of the Magnate if he's noticed any drunk vampires wandering around. It's a dumbass question, and the last thing I need is to look incompetent in front of someone who sleeps with a sword under his pillow. I opt for lunch with Derrick instead.

The restaurant is busy. Every couple in the city must be craving expensive cocktails. I find him sitting by the window.

"Who did you blow to get this table?"

"Good afternoon to you, too."

I sit down. "Thanks for the invite. I'm starving."

"I took a chance and ordered you the three-cheese burger."

"Good call."

A model/waiter brings our food. We eat in semi-silence, which is one of the perks of having a best friend who can read your thoughts. Right now, I'm grappling with the realization that this cheese is going to give me gas. Once I've resigned myself to that, I start thinking about Lucian again.

"He asked me about you," Derrick says.

"What do you mean?"

"Lucian. We were talking at breakfast—while you were snoring—and he asked me if something was up with you."

I bristle slightly. "Why not just ask me himself?"

"Because you're the Death Star deflector shield."

"Oh, *I'm* the deflector? Have you talked to Selena yet?"

He looks around, as if CORE agents are everywhere. "For your information," he says, lowering his voice, "I did."

"And?"

"And what?"

"Is Miles going to be questioned?"

"Of course not. He has nothing to do with this."

"He could have been at the scene, and you know it."

"Actually, I know that he has no reason to hang around Burnaby Mountain in the middle of the night."

"Actually, McBitchy, he has a life of his own. You have no idea if he was meeting with you-know-who or not."

"He would have told me."

"Just like you've told him about the time you used thought-control to get him to return that late movie? Or is that still a secret?"

"I—" He reddens slightly. "That hasn't come up yet."

I fold my arms. "You need to tell him. And Miles needs to be questioned. He's a big boy. I'm sure he can handle whatever Selena's going to ask him."

"She said it sounded circumstantial."

"Are you kidding? She loves circumstantial."

He stares at his empty plate. "Why would he have been talking to you-know-who? The two literally live in separate worlds."

"The last time I checked, spatial profilers were sort of known for prying into other worlds. Do you really know everywhere he's been?"

"No," he says sullenly. "Do you know everywhere that Lucian's been?"

"Of course not."

We're both silent for a while.

Derrick sighs. "I need another Bellini."

"I'm already on it."

5

After nightfall, I head to the vampire community
center. Patrick's at home, so I know that Modred will be
there by himself. Even though he saved my life once, I'm
still not sure how much I can trust him. Patrick thinks he
hung the moon and the stars. I'm a bit of a harder sell.
When I reach the nondescript entrance, I ring the buzzer,
which is new. A girl opens the door. She looks about my
age, but the red flecks in her eyes suggest that she's been
around for quite a bit longer.

"I'm Tess Corday." I incline my head, which seems
only polite. "I'm here to talk with Modred."

"He's in a mood."

"Would you call it a bloodlust mood, or just general
snark?"

"You can see for yourself. Don't be surprised if he won't talk to you, though. He's been ignoring everyone the whole night."

She ushers me into the common area. A few vampires are watching TV, while others play cards at a makeshift table. There's a line for the computer, as always. I head upstairs to Patrick's office. It's odd to think that the kid who still watches *DuckTales* also commands every vampire in the city of Vancouver. He loves me, as much as an immortal can love anything, but I also know that he'd take me apart if he had to. Sometimes, when I walk by his bedroom and hear him gently snoring, I think: *He's yours, and he's a killer.*

Modred sits at Patrick's desk. He's studying paperwork and doesn't look up when I come in. "Tess. What brings you here?"

"I have a question for you."

"I have answered a dozen of the Magnate's questions today, and I doubt that he absorbed a single thing. If I answer you, will you listen?"

"As I suspected," I say. "General snark."

"Excuse me?"

"Never mind."

Modred looks up at me. His lip ring is a half-moon against pale flesh. There are bags under his eyes. He looks like a photosensitive teenager, like one of those scary orphans from the horror movie with Nicole Kidman. I don't know how old he is really, but he does have an

Anglo-Saxon vibe, which leads me to believe that he spent time chilling with Manticores and purebloods. Certainly he knew Caitlyn, the former Magnate who sired Patrick. I should be more nervous around him, but we bonded during a cab ride, or at least I think we did. Plus, disarticulating me will tick off Patrick, and Modred is nothing if not loyal.

"What is your question, Tess?"

"It's about vampires getting drunk."

"You came all the way here to ask me about that? Vampires get drunk the same way humans do, only it takes more alcohol. Mead often does the trick."

"I saw a vampire who looked—I don't know—blissed out. Kind of drunk, but kind of not. How would a drunk vampire behave?"

His expression changes. "Who else have you asked about this?"

"I don't know his name. The bouncer at Blood Drive."

"Is this how you conduct an investigation? You simply hail vampires on the street and ask them random questions?"

"I'm off duty, actually."

"Ah." He motions for me to sit down next to him. "So you want to combat idleness by investigating pointless things."

I sit. "It sounds better in my head."

"What was so strange about this drunken vampire that you saw?"

"I don't know. There was just something off about him."

"Wait here," he says. "I have something to show you."

He leaves and comes back with a DVD, which he puts in the player. He turns on the TV. I see Patrick sitting on the couch downstairs, along with a bunch of other vampires that I don't recognize. They're all singing in some language that I can't understand. Patrick chugs his beer. Then he opens his mouth and belches so loud that it shakes the furniture on camera. Everyone laughs.

Modred turns off the TV. "That is a drunk vampire," he says. "Did the one you saw behave like that?"

"Not at all. He seemed devious. And hungry."

"Did he attack you?"

"No. I flashed a bit of power, and he backed off. But the next day, I saw him out with a group of his friends. It seemed bold. He didn't go after me, but he made sure I knew that he was watching."

"If he is that careless, I cannot see him living for too much longer. If I were you, I would turn your mind to more important matters."

"I'm on leave, remember? I can't involve myself in important matters. It's either check this out or go for the all-time best score on Freecell."

"I can see how that might drive you to distraction." He looks at the paperwork again, then shudders. "I suppose we both could use something interesting to occupy us. How would you feel about attending a party tomorrow night?"

"A vampire party?"

"More or less. The crowd will mostly be young and stupid, but you may run into your bold friend."

"I'd feel a bit like Lady Gaga when she wore the meat dress."

"I have no idea what you're talking about."

"I'd be on display."

"I'll be with you. Nothing can happen."

"Knock on wood."

"What?"

"It's customary to knock on wood after you say nothing bad will happen. You've probably been dead too long to remember, but it makes everyone feel better." I knock lightly on the surface of the desk. "See? Now you do it."

Modred stares at me as if I've deeply disappointed him. Then he knocks three times, with deliberation. He puts his ear to the desk.

"Who is supposed to answer?" he asks.

"No one. It's like whistling in the dark."

"Whistling in the dark is sonar."

I sigh. "It's a propitiatory custom, like lighting a candle or wearing a talisman. I guess it's meant to remind us not to take anything for granted."

He continues to listen to the desk. "I hear atoms," he says. "Nothing more."

"What time are you picking me up tomorrow?"

"Midnight."

"Fine. I'll wear a turtleneck."

* * *

Against my better judgment, I take a bus to Fourth
Avenue and Vine. The posh stores have gone to sleep, but
the bars and cafés remain aglow. Kitsilano is the land of
joggers clad in formfitting Lululemon shorts, a place
where, as Douglas Coupland observed, even the dogs have
sweaters. The streets are filled with wandering prides of
undergrads looking for drink specials. I avoid them and
head to the Pleasure Box, an adult video store that shares
space with CORE clinic 21B. The mannequins in the
window seem to be having a good time. The blacked-out
door chimes when I open it. A bored woman looks up
from the counter, nods at me, then returns to her book. I
walk past the rows of videos and sex toys with their lewd
Japanese packaging. A nondescript door in the back leads
to a flight of steps, which takes me to the clinic.

It's a busy night. Several young people are being treated
for materia burn. Someone or something howls behind a
set of flowered curtains. I approach the front desk and ask
the nurse on duty if Evelyn is working tonight.

"She just went for coffee. She'll be back in fifteen."

I take a seat in the waiting room. The chairs are the
color of Habitant pea soup, and look as if they were donated
from St. Paul's. I wonder, not for the first time, how the
CORE manages to keep all of this running. I suppose if
the Templars were able to spread their influence across
Europe and Asia, it stands to reason that people who can

channel materia would be able to sustain a global corporation. But who started it? Nobody knows. Probably not even Esther. Maybe it was Merlin. The thought makes me laugh in spite of myself. A sullen goblin with a head wound glares at me. I smother my laughter and stare at the linoleum.

Derrick and I took Mia to this very clinic after we were attacked by a Vailoid demon, basically a man-shark. Killing him was messy. Afterward, we all sat around here, sedately drinking our juice boxes and trying to joke about what had just happened. I'd like to think that we made her feel better, but I remember the look in her eyes too well. She'd seen magic, and wanted to bury it, to run from it. I'd felt that way once. But now magic was just like red wine and cigarettes, something warmly inescapable that gave pleasure even as it exacted a familiar price.

"Tess?"

I look up. Evelyn is standing there, holding a to-go cup from Blenz.

"Hey. I have a question for you."

"I'm about to start my second shift. Is this the sort of question that you need to ask in private?"

"It is."

"Okay. Follow me."

She takes me down a hallway marked with red and blue intersecting lines. Gurneys lie forgotten in the corners. It reminds me of a dream I had once, which ended in my father's face becoming bloody wax. I suppose that was Arcadia's touch. *I wanted you to hate him like I did,* she told me. What she hadn't realized was that her counterfeit nightmares would fan my curiosity instead. Why the bones, the sand castles, the dripping tap? Maybe it all meant something to her.

We step into an empty exam room. Evelyn shuts the door. She puts down her coffee and gives me a long look.

"I know why you're here."

"You do?"

"There's only one question that would bring you down here, alone, in the middle of the night. But I don't have an answer for you."

"Tell me it wasn't a car accident," I say.

"I only know what she told me."

"What she told you to write on the report, you mean."

"Her injuries were consistent—"

"Evelyn, please. I'm not stupid. If it had been a car accident, she wouldn't have gone to a CORE clinic."

"It was—" She shakes her head. "There was a normate with her. The guy wouldn't leave her side, but she couldn't very well tell him the truth."

"But she told you."

"She had a concussion. She was barely coherent."

"She must have said something about what attacked her."

"Why don't you just ask her?"

"Don't you think I have? She just lies. Her lies are complicated, beautiful, like layer cakes. I can't cut through them."

"There's a reason that she doesn't want you to know."

"Did you do an assault kit?"

"Tess, I can't answer that."

"Was there evidence of trauma?"

Evelyn calmly picks up her coffee and opens the door. "I promised her that I would never tell anyone. I'm sorry."

Sadness crawls into my throat. I blink. "Do you know what it's like," I whisper, "not knowing where you came from?"

Evelyn pauses with her hand on the door. For a moment, I see pain flash across her eyes. When she speaks, her voice is barely audible. "She wanted Rhophylac."

She walks out before I can respond.

I can't catch my breath. I'm wheezing as I leave the clinic. Outside, a warm rain has begun. I can't stand still. I have to run. I pass the intersection of Fourth and Vine and keep running, until I hit the beach. This was where we found Ru. We thought he was dead, but he woke up on the autopsy table, like a small scaly miracle. The sand clutches at my feet, but I keep running awkwardly. When I reach the dark water, I drop to my knees and retch.

My phone begins to vibrate. I look at the call display. It's Derrick. I try to answer, but all I can do is sob weakly.

"Tess? What's going on?"

"She—" The bile rises in my throat again. "She knew. Derrick, she knew all along, but she—she—"

"Sweetheart, where are you?"

I hang up.

My hands are trembling. Slowly, I get to my feet. The cold water soaks my canvas shoes. The moon is a pitiless cat's eye. I stare at the obscure waves until I can't feel my toes anymore. Then I turn around and start back up the beach. In the distance, I can see an LED light flashing. A late-night runner or cyclist, immune to family drama, committed to fitness. The thought almost makes me smile.

I feel another cold that has nothing to do with my wet shoes. All I can do is laugh softly. Of course a fucking vampire would find me, tonight of all nights, wrecked and crying on a beach. It's practically operatic. I pull out my athame. The blade is a bare suggestion of silver in the dark.

"Come out," I say. "Or run. I don't care. But don't think for a second that I'm some little rabbit for you to gnaw on. I've got teeth just like you."

The vampire from the convenience store appears. He has his hands in his pockets, like he's just taking an innocuous stroll. His eyes are red and cloudy. He smells strange. When he sees my athame, he smiles. His teeth are stained wine dark.

"Who are you?" I raise the dagger. "I'm not playing."

"I thought you people loved to play."

I frown. "What people?"

"You're CORE."

"Right. Sure, we can be Byzantine, I guess. But what you seem to be forgetting is that your people and mine have a truce."

He steps closer. "The truce ended with him."

"I'm not sure you understand what a truce is. Lord Nightingale's death hasn't affected the law. If you attack me, you'll be punished."

"I'm not afraid of pain."

"Oh, no? One of the downsides of being undead is that torture kind of takes on a whole new dimension."

"When I'm finished drinking, there won't even be enough dry pieces of you left for the wind to carry away."

I assume a defensive stance. "You know what's sad? That's not even the worst pickup line I've ever heard."

He moves quickly. Too quickly for a whelp. Maybe I was wrong about his age. I slam the pommel of my athame into his mouth, shattering one of his molars. He swears and spits out blood, which is the same color as the black water. I reach for a strand of earth materia and let it slip into the blade, which becomes a singing blue candle. I level it at the vampire.

"I've been fighting your people since I was thirteen. You think you can intimidate me? I've looked into the eyes of a Manticore. I stabbed an Iblis, right in the middle of his flaming fontanels. You're nothing but a drunk moron."

He leaps. His feet push him off the sand, like the beach is his trampoline. He slams into me, and we both fall into the water. The shock of the cold makes me gasp. Before I can move, his hands are around my throat. It takes only a few pounds of pressure to strangle someone, and he has the strength of an insane wrestler who's tweaking on PCP.

I start to see spots. My athame is in the water. I search for it, but my numb fingers find only wet sand and lichen.

He leans in closer. That's the nice thing about vampires. They love what they do a bit too much. The desire makes them vulnerable. When he's close enough for me to smell his breath, I reach up and drive my thumb into his right eye. I push hard, until the sclera yields and warm fluid bathes my hand. The eye breaks like a split fruit. He screams, and the pressure around my throat lessens, enough for me to kick him and crawl away. My wet hand comes down on something hard in the water, and I pull out the athame, still shining.

"I'm not sure how the vampiric healing factor works, exactly," I say, "but I feel like it's going to take a while for you to grow a new eyeball."

He stands up. His face is covered in blood. He screams a word that I can't understand, then runs at me again. I spin to the side and slash just above his kneecap, opening the popliteal artery. A fan of blood soaks my jeans. Why do I never think to wear a damn slicker until it's too late?

He howls and reaches for me. I kick him in the chest. He stumbles, but keeps coming. It's not as if vampires have a lot of blood in them, and he's already leaking like a sprinkler. Why is he so stubborn?

I slash again, aiming for another artery—a nice brachial one—but he catches my wrist. His hand moves swiftly. I feel a bloom of pain, as if someone has just set fire to my hand. I drop the athame. My brain registers the fact that my wrist is broken, but for a second, all I can do is stand there, like a cartoon coyote, perplexed by the impact of the falling anvil. Still holding on to my broken wrist, he pulls me to him. The pain makes me sick. He grabs my hair and yanks my head back, exposing my throat.

"You have beautiful circulation," he says.

I stare at the moon. The fire trick won't work this time, not in the middle of the ocean. Water is my mother's element, not mine. But she's also inside of me, just like he is. For every demonic protein running rampant through my body, there's a piece of my mother, a mitochondrial knight streaming along embattled vessels. The water in my blood calls to the water around me.

I feel the something coalesce in my hand. A stinger of ice. A blade of astonished liquid, seaweed, and shell matrix, which I drive through his heart.

He stumbles back with the icicle stuck in his chest. Blood streams from his mouth, nose, and eyes. He's laughing, but the sound is like rent cloth. His skin is already beginning to slough off. His fingers curl as they decompose. I smell the sweet reek of cadaverine, the tincture of decay, as it spreads through him.

"You don't even know." He laughs. "You idiot. You don't even know what's going on. That's the funniest thing of all."

"Tell me, then. What are you on? What was the point of this?"

"He'll destroy you."

"Oh, please. Did Arcadia put you up to this? Look, I know that my father is a crazy mofo, but this is getting old."

He falls to his knees. His face is mostly gone now, a steaming crater of broken tesserae.

"Who sent you?"

He melts into the water. Seconds later, there's nothing left of him but smoke and a vile odor. I start to shake. I can barely feel my broken wrist, which means that my body is going into shock. Numbly, I make my way back into the beach, holding my injured hand close to my chest. I see headlights. I hear voices. Someone is running toward me, and I realize that it's Derrick.

"She's here! I've got her!"

He sees the blood on me. He sees my wrist. Before he can say anything, I bury my face in his neck and start to cry.

"I've got you," he whispers. "Geez. What happened? Did a shark attack you? What are you doing here at this time of night?"

"I don't know," I say, holding on to him. "I don't know who's lying to me and who isn't. I can't fucking tell anymore."

"I'll never lie to you again."

I want to believe him, but I can't. I look down and see a glimmer of light on the sand. It's my athame, burning like a birthday candle too stubborn to realize that its peculiar life is already over.

6

This is an old dream.

I'm in the pool with my mother. She spins me around in circles while I exclaim: *I love my friend the water.* I make waves with my small, prunish hands, while she holds me. I whirl in the heart of a golden mean. I am an overjoyed crystal in my mother's arms, polished by the sun and the water.

I know that she will never let me go. We will spin like an eternal record in this flood, and after, on the drive home, I will eat a tuna sandwich with diced pickles and watch the trees effervesce. With my bare feet propped against the cooler, I can drift with the power lines as my mother sings us around familiar curves in the road. A blue spark glows in my hand. I look at it and smile. It's a burning flake of our water I stole when nobody was looking.

I open my eyes. I'm in my own bed, doused in sweat. For a moment, the loss of the dream is so sharp that I can feel its exit wound. Then I realize that it's just my fractured wrist, numbed by painkillers but still throbbing. I look up at the ceiling fan. All it can do is displace the muggy air. My sheets are a wet tangle. I could take a shower, but I can't bear the thought of more water. I can still see the vampire melting before me like a hideous snowflake.

I don't think that my father sent him. But if not my father, then who? Arcadia? She could kill me by blinking if she wanted to. She had no reason to send tweaked vampires after me.

I can't stop thinking about what he said. *The truce ended with him.* If this is the public sentiment among vampires, then something has gone seriously wrong. Deonara isn't doing her job as the new Lord Nightingale. I doubt I'll have any luck brokering a meeting with her, but I can at least ask Modred about it. Figuring out what to wear to an undead house party will distract me from thinking about what I learned at the clinic.

I pull on a clean shirt and walk into the living room. Derrick's watching television, and he frowns when he sees me.

"You should be asleep."

"It's too hot. The fan is useless."

"Those painkillers are hard on your stomach." He stands up. "I'll get you some dry toast and ginger ale."

"You don't have to."

"Nonsense. I'll be back in two shakes of a rabbit's tail."

I sit down on the couch. It's so late that it might as well be morning. They spent hours fussing over me, plying me with hot tea and blankets. It was a relief when everyone finally went to bed. I've never liked being taken care of. I'm like a cat when I'm sick. All I want to do is crawl under a piece of furniture and sleep.

Derrick returns with a plate of dry toast and a glass of ginger ale. He places them warily next to me, as if I might claw him. The bubbles relax me, but it's hard to chew because my throat still aches.

"What are you watching?" I ask, once I've finished.

"*Today's Special.* For some reason, they air it late at night."

"I used to have a crush on the mannequin guy."

"Didn't we all?"

I lie down with my head in his lap. He dabs at the sweat on my forehead with his sleeve. His fingers are cool. His Canucks pajamas are worn and smell like a dryer sheet. We're silent for a while. Puppets dance on the television, while outside, darkness presses the world into familiar shapes.

"What were you doing on that beach?"

His voice stirs me. I've been expecting that question

all night, but only now, in this anchorite silence, is he able to ask me.

"I was at the clinic," I say. "I had to talk to Evelyn."

"About what?"

"Derrick—" I stare at the classic skate logo on his pajamas. "I don't think my mother was raped. I think she was already pregnant when Kevin found her. Those injuries were caused by something else entirely."

He touches my hair lightly. "How do you know that?"

"Evelyn said that she asked for Rhophylac. That drug is used in cases where a Rhesus incompatibility factor might develop in the mother's blood. She would have only asked for the injection if she knew"—I swallow—"that our blood was at odds. Which makes sense, given what my father is."

"Why would she lie to you?"

"I don't know."

"So—what?—your stepdad found her that night, and she just pretended that she'd been assaulted by someone?"

"She was hurt. She must have been fighting something. If she'd been thinking clearly, maybe she never would have let Kevin come with her to the clinic. Maybe we never would have met him. Isn't it weird how random life can be? If he hadn't walked past that parking lot, he never would have entered our lives."

"Are you going to talk to her?"

"I don't know what to say. *Hey, Mom, any particular reason why you fuzzied up the details of my conception?*

She'll just say that she was protecting me. That's her answer for everything."

"It's kind of her job. Wouldn't you do the same for Mia?"

"I wouldn't lie to her about something so important."

"What if the truth were a hundred times worse?"

I sigh. "It almost always is."

"Do you want some more toast?"

"No, thank you."

"Are you tired?"

I yawn. "Maybe."

"Try to sleep."

"What are you going to do?"

"Keep watching. I want to know how this episode ends."

"Jeff turns back into a mannequin."

"I know that. But Muffy the Mouse is up to something. I feel like it's all about to get pretty wild."

I feel weightless. Everything flutters down, and the last thing I hear is Derrick asking me why I think TXL Series 4 is such an uptight computer. Then I sink back into the water. She's let go, but I can float on my own, enchanted by the bones and black pearls that surround us.

Most of my morning is taken up by a bizarre interview with Selena and Patrick. As Magnate, he has to be present while I'm debriefed about the incident on the beach with the psychotic vampire. I tell them both everything that happened, beginning with the first time I noticed him at the convenience store, and ending with how his body disappeared into the water. "Like sugar dissolving into tea," I almost say, but hold back. Neither of them is particularly into similes. Patrick writes nothing down. He's angry about the attack, but that's the extent of his interest. It would have been more helpful to have Modred here— at least he might have something to offer—but the last thing I want to do is offend Patrick. He can be surprisingly touchy.

After the debriefing is over, he gives me a hug and promises to buy groceries. I don't believe him, but the hug is nice. I say nothing about the vampire house party, which I still plan to attend. If he knew about it, he'd insist on coming as my man-at-arms, but his presence would only arouse suspicion. Modred is slicker. Derrick isn't happy that I want to, in his words, "dive into a vampire orgy" after what happened on the beach, but this is my best chance to gather information. Looking tired and beat-up will only make me less attractive to them, anyhow.

Selena takes me to the break room for a coffee. I haven't been here in a while, and I feel a bit imposterish, like an overage prom date. Still, the coffee smells every bit as unpalatable as I remember. We sit on the couch in silence, waiting for our respective mugs to cool. In the hallway, I can hear Linus complaining about the eyepiece on his scanning electron microscope.

"What is your problem?" Selena asks. Her tone is so

gentle that the words don't register at first. I give her an odd look.

"Am I only allowed to have one?"

"I'm serious. You're supposed to be on mental-health leave. This is your time to figure things out—as in, do you want this job, or don't you? Instead, I find you tangling with vampires on Kits Beach."

"Tangling? Are you saying that I asked for it?"

"No. I'm saying you should have been at home with your family. What's so hard about relaxing for once?"

"I'm sorry; have we met? I'm wound tightly. You know that."

"What do you want to do?"

"I'm not sure I understand the question."

"I'm not talking metaphysically. What do you want to do with your life right now, at this moment? Do you want to retire, or do you want to keep working for the CORE? You can't have it both ways."

"I never thought retirement was an option."

"Look—" Selena puts her hand on mine. It may be the first time she's ever touched me. "You've done a lot. Your accomplishments haven't gone unnoticed. If you want to walk away from this, I'm authorized to sign your retirement papers. You'd have a generous pension. You'd be free."

"Free? That word means nothing for people like us."

"Maybe you don't really want to leave."

"What would I do? Garden? Take up capoeira? I'd still

see vampires around every corner. I'd still hear the rocks and the trees swearing at me. The only difference is that I'd have to pretend to be normal."

"Would that really be so bad?"

I shake my head. "Mia's about to leave for college. Patrick's mostly gone already, and it's only a matter of time before Derrick and Miles decide to shack up together. Who exactly would I be doing this for?"

"You."

I stand up. "There's no such person."

"Tess."

"Thank you, Selena. I get what you're offering me, and I'm not trying to throw it back in your face. But I just don't know."

"I'll need an answer from you eventually."

"I understand that." I drain the mug. "Thank you for the coffee, and for everything else that you've given me. I know I can be difficult."

"That's why I like you."

"I do have one question."

"What's that?"

"How did the interview with Miles Sedgwick go?"

She considers the question for a moment. Technically, it's vague enough that I'm not overstepping any boundaries.

"It was inconclusive. That's all I can say."

"Fair enough."

"Take care, Tess. Call me if you decide anything."

"I will. I promise."

The air-conditioning in the lobby raises gooseflesh on my arms. I walk to Waterfront Station. I know I should call my mother, but I can't bring myself to dial her number. I'm afraid of what I might say. A part of me realizes that she has every right to her privacy, and that the lie she told me was most likely a merciful one. But that realization has done nothing to diminish my anger. I'm not even sure who I'm mad at anymore, to be honest. At the moment, I want to punch the SkyTrain for being late.

I'm a damp mess by the time I get home. I take a lukewarm bath, argue with my hair for a bit, and then put on a robe and slippers. I grab a beer from the fridge and nurse it while sitting on the patio. If anyone ever thought my private life was sexy, the image of me in a terry-cloth robe drinking PBR should disabuse them of that notion. My legs are smooth and moisturized, but there's nobody around to touch them. I think about calling Lucian, but it seems like a bad idea. He knows me too well. One look at my face, and he'll ask me what happened. I don't want to tell the story of the melting vampire again. I just want a little action. It doesn't seem like so much to ask.

Andy Warhol said that there should be a course on love in the first grade. Most of the time, I feel like I'm in relationship preschool. I'm still working with blunted scissors and paste. Lucian understands romance, while my idea of a fine night together is sharing a bag of Hawkins Cheezies in bed while watching *Flight of the*

Conchords. I'm not sure if I should be putting in more effort, but he doesn't seem to mind. He's unflappable, which started out being sexy, but now it's just cryptic. When I look at Derrick and Miles, it seems like being a couple just comes naturally to them. It makes me suspect that they've taken some kind of continuing-ed class. I brought this up with Lucian once, and he said: *They just fit.* I wanted to ask if we fit, or if maybe we needed a shoehorn, but instead I just laughed because Jemaine was pole dancing.

I was thirteen when I learned that I could see and touch materia. While most girls my age were having sleepovers and hanging out at the mall, I was learning how to fight with a dagger and make stones dance. People like me have the most power when we're young, and the CORE knows that. We're bright burning weapons. Those of us who choose to work in the field learn to trust our training, but all those bitter lessons are also a form of control. I realize now that I was taught to channel materia in specific ways, and although that knowledge has kept me alive, I don't always agree with it. When you tell a power *do this*, it responds grudgingly. It assumes the shape that you've requested, but after a while, the exercise becomes rote. I can't remember the last time I pulled a Schmendrick and just said to the power: *Do what you will.*

I close my eyes and let down my aegis. I don't search for anything in particular. I just send out a general invitation. Powers are cagey. Like rabbits, they need you to keep still and avert your gaze. I try to think about nothing. I surrender to entropy as it gnaws at the corners of my life. Protein by protein, my helices grind down; my sunburned myelin flakes. I accept this. Decay makes artful music.

For a moment, I'm somewhere else. I put out my hands and touch something, an edge that cuts my fingers. *Careful,* my father's voice says. *You're too young to know this yet, but some worlds have thorns.*

I open my eyes. I don't know how long I've been sitting here, but my tailbone aches; my muscles are sore. It hardly feels fair that just meditating should exact a toll on the body. I make some coffee and then Derrick phones.

"I'm taking a long lunch at Granville Park. You need to help me find a shady spot for Patrick. You know how particular he is."

I shower, put on a sundress, and leave the house. The park is full of dogs wearing bandannas. Derrick has spread out a blanket under a tree with aggressive roots. The leaves deflect most of the sunlight, but Patrick still has his hood up, and I can smell the Banana Boat lotion on his hands. Mia is texting someone, her eyes narrowed in concentration, and I wonder, not for the first time, how much of our brains are devoted to cycling rapidly through menus and petting track pads. Miles offers me a cream soda. He's wearing the blue shirt that Derrick likes. He's met Lord Nightingale; I'm almost certain of it. When Selena calls something "inconclusive," it's usually because it was too weird for her to articulate. I take the can and hug him. Oh, Miles, I love you. I love your quietude and the weft of your hands. I love to watch you dance through the alphabet. When Derrick looks at you, I hear the scratch of his love on your floor.

I sit down next to Patrick. At least he's untroubled by mosquitoes. There's a family seated close by. Their bubble machine has attracted a small crowd. They don't look that different from us, although we have no props, just a cooler. I smell pot and citronella candles. We're about to break out the sandwiches when, suddenly, all the leashless dogs part to admit Lady Duessa and Wolfie. Most of the people here are normates, so they have no idea how powerful both of them are. We push our blankets together. Duessa kisses my cheek, then pulls a cherry-cheese Danish out of her clutch and hands it to me, perfectly preserved. She smells like vetiver.

I could ask her about Lord Nightingale, but she won't tell me what I really need to know. She's too smart. She and the Iblis used to crash the same parties. I try to imagine how old she must be. Surely as old as Mr. Corvid, who rocked the Bronze Age. When I look at Duessa, I see a social being with a perilous core. She's smiling now, but technically, she could eat all of us.

Derrick sees my Danish and makes his move. I give him half, which is the standard pastry tithe in our relationship. Derrick, it was you who saved me. You paged Katie Green, whose gremlin roared in her purse, who invited me to her party even though she suspected I was mentally disabled. Katie Green, who'd known no magic other than the indefatigable power of her credit card. Derrick, it was you who went upstairs with me, you who let me kiss you, even though you didn't normally kiss girls. But there was a Boyz II Men poster on the wall, and it all seemed good. It was you who walked with me past the electric paintbrush at the edge of the water. You promised we would be like sea turtles, and I guess we have been, our shells collecting striae.

It was you who introduced me to latkes. It was you who cosigned our mortgage. Derrick, please keep being my Rosetta Stone. Please continue shredding my old BC Hydro envelopes. Please don't stop buying sponges. Derrick, oh, Derrick, don't go. You can't. Who will I be without you? What will your absence sound like? Will it be the nullity of a spent capillary? No. It will be the universe on fire, its patios ashing away, its escapes howling like mutilated kettles, and Leonard Cohen won't be there, Manu Chao won't be there, coffee won't be there, naked boys won't be there, Saturn's Cassini Division won't be there, but I will, so thank you and fuck you for having a plan when I never did. Miles will make interesting soups for you. Miles will let you read his thoughts, because they're clean. Fuck you, Miles, for having such clean thoughts.

Everyone, stay. Mia, stay; I have so much to talk to you about, so many ways to embarrass you with my dog love. I'll buy you a new SIM card. I'll give you more counter space, scads of it, without borders, I promise. You can be a vampire. You can kill me if you need to, as long as you stay. Mia, *margarita*, my fang and flower. I am not as swift or as keen-sighted as other mothers. I have hesitated when I should have taken your hand. I have dragged death into your life. I have allowed you to keep odd hours and drink too much caffeine. But, Mia, if you could see what my love looks like, it might stop you, like an accident or fireworks.

Much later, I text Modred and ask him to meet me for pre-drinks at Sawbones. The last time I attended a vampire party, the keg was named Tim. That's fine if you're a vampire, but I really just wanted a Keith's. I take a bus to Gastown, which is a hot mess full of club kids and drunken tourists. I was never so adventurous. I took my top off at Shine once, but I was cleaning it in the bathroom, so that doesn't count.

Sawbones is mellow when I get there. The necromancers are sitting in their usual corner booth. They don't quite glare at me when I walk in, but they manage to look chilly. I ignore them. Most likely, they disapprove of my relationship with Lucian. Or maybe they're just scared shitless because Theresa's death has left a power vacuum. Like vampires, they can be hard to read until it's too late.

I sit at the only clean table I can find. There are two goblins in a vinyl booth across from me, and they're staring. I can't tell if they're a couple, or just friends. One of them whispers something that I can't understand. I want to tell them to keep their Skeksi-like speculations to themselves, but I don't need to draw any more attention. I order a pint of Rickard's and wait for Modred. This place used to freak me out, but once the clientele saw me talking to Lady Duessa, they learned not to hassle me. You don't cross someone who dresses in weak nuclear force.

Modred comes through the door. He's wearing slacks and a smart blazer. I wonder for a second if he's become one of the Warblers. He sits down and does his best to smile. It comes out as a polite grimace. Normally, it would take more muscles to frown than to smile, but not if you're dead. The waitress notices him, but doesn't approach our table. Vampires tend to order from the bar anyhow.

"Are you having anything?"

"No," he replies. "I will drink at the party."

"Right."

"Do not imbibe too much. It will dull your senses, and the last thing you want is to be caught off guard."

"I thought you were protecting me."

"I cannot be everywhere at once."

"What's that called again? Bilocation?"

"There may be a few older ones there who can do that. Watch out for them. Always keep your back to the wall."

"Ah. It's like I'm in college again."

Unexpectedly, he touches my face. "You are slightly anemic. You must be careful. Stay hydrated and keep your guard up."

"You must be exciting on a date."

"Vampires do not date. We mate. At times, we cohabit, but that is mostly for protection. Only humans subject themselves to such social agony."

"Sure. The dating scene would be a lot more progressive if we all just ate each other anonymously, like civilized demons."

"Precisely."

I finish my second drink and Modred pays the bill, which is nice of him. I hate when vampires try to pull that whole *I don't carry cash because I'm ageless* bullshit. We take a cab to the party, which is in Shaugnessey. Trees bow beneath the weight of the neighborhood's largesse. Signs decorate the Chinese consulate building. We get off at the corner of West Eighty-seventh and walk to the house, a standard late-seventies bungalow whose lawn has been brought up-to-date. Two vampires meet us at the door. Modred simply looks at them, and they let us by (although one of them rakes my ass with his eyes).

The living room is packed with all sorts: humans, demihumans, semi-friendly monsters, and an inchoate bartender. There are goblins on the couch, sharing a joint and a bowl of dried fruit. A few people are dancing in various states of undress. I cast my senses out like a net, dragging the room. Everything, alive or undead, has a unique print. Sort of like an aura, but funkier. The goblins are topaz lights that remind me of indolent glowworms; the vampires move in cold flashes, dropping carnelian sparks that dance with them. I look at Modred, and it's clear that he's the oldest thing in the room. He burns like a bed of coals.

Modred taps one of the dancing vampires on the shoulder. *"Hwelp,"* he says, *"hwær es eower cwene?"*

"Dude, what are you talking about?"

He sighs. "Where is the lady of the house?"

"You mean Quartilla? I think she's in the kitchen."

Modred turns to me. "I'll go talk to her. Mingle, but do not touch."

"Don't worry. This isn't my first rodeo."

"I have no idea what that could mean, but I will return."

He moves through the crowd and vanishes into the kitchen. I walk over to the bar, which is really just a table covered in sweating bottles of vermouth. The bartender is semiopaque. I think she might be a phasma. I watch her mix a mojito, which she gives to one of the goblins. He drops a toonie into a jar full of change. She may be a ghost, but she's making great tips.

She turns to me and asks: *"Qui potus volas, amica?"*

"I'm sorry. I don't speak Latin."

"What would you like?"

"A scotch and soda."

"Coming right up."

I drop a twenty into the change jar. Without looking up from mixing my drink, she says sweetly: "Twenty gets you a heart-warming story. If you actually want me to answer a question, it's going to cost you."

"How much?"

"A kiss."

I consider this for a second. I've never been proposi-
tioned by a phasma before. She is pretty, despite the fact
that I can see through her.

"Fine. Don't steal my soul, though."

"I'll only take a crumb."

We kiss. I feel pins and needles in my mouth. True to
her word, she steals barely a flake from me, but I'm still
left light-headed. She smiles and hands me the drink.
"That was nice. You've had an interesting life."

"Yeah. I've always been a bit touched."

"Plane-walkers. Manticores. Necromancers. You're
like an occult fire sale."

"That's a strange compliment, but I'll take it."

"So what do you want to know?"

I tell her about the amped-up vampire who attacked
me. I try to make it sound like a mugging that just happened to take place in the water. I keep my voice low, lest
the dancing vampires overhear me.

"Vampires don't usually drink," she says. "It's one of
many reasons that they're bad for business. However,
there are a few intense barbiturates that can get a vampire
really strung out."

"Like Hex?"

The phasma casts a glance around the room. Then she
leans in close, as if to kiss me again, and says: "Pharmakon."

Before I can ask her what this is, something vaguely eldritch walks up to the bar and orders a Chi-Chi. The phasma sighs and reaches for the pineapple juice. I guess I shouldn't be surprised. Even at a party like this, a kiss can buy you only so much.

I make my way into the kitchen. Modred is talking to a beautiful vampire with short black hair. They're speaking Anglo-Saxon, and all the fricative consonants give them a chance to exercise their fangs. When she sees me, she smiles, and switches to faintly accented English. Her cuff links, I realize, are finger bones.

"Hello, child. Welcome to my home."

I incline my head. "Thank you, Quartilla."

"How do you know Modred?"

"He saved me from a crazy necromancer."

She rolls her eyes. "We've all been there."

Modred looks at me. "Are you ready to go?"

"I think so. It's getting late."

Quartilla frowns slightly. "You smell curious."

"I've been told that before."

Modred suddenly grabs my hand. "We had best be going. It was lovely talking to you, Quartilla."

"Of course. The pleasure was mine."

Modred doesn't let go of my hand until we're outside. Then he takes a step back, looking almost embarrassed.

"Sorry. I was trying to mask your scent with mine."

"I don't know how to respond to that. Thank you?"

"I did not want Quartilla to smell the Magnate on you.

If she knew that the two of you were connected, she might take an unhealthy interest in you."

"Right. That makes sense. Did you learn anything from her?"

"Nothing I did not already know. There are always newly sired whelps running around, wreaking havoc, but she has not seen anything untoward."

"What's Pharmakon?"

He looks angry. "Who spoke of this?"

"A phasma with a bit of a crush on me."

He relaxes slightly but still looks annoyed. "It's an elixir. It can act as a powerful opiate, but very few understand the distillation process. Some don't even believe that it exists. You can't believe everything a dead bartender tells you."

"What's it made from?"

"You do not want to know."

"Awesome."

Modred puts a hand on my shoulder. "Ask no one about this. Do you understand? It is forbidden. Anyone who knows about it will kill you the moment the word 'Pharmakon' leaves your lips."

"That doesn't leave me with a lot of options."

"I will make some inquiries, but I cannot promise anything."

"Why do I feel like you're managing me?"

He says nothing.

"Fine. Tell me why it's forbidden, at least. It's not like vampires are morally queasy about most things."

"The less you know about it, the better. I brought you with me so that I could keep an eye on you. I don't want you wandering around asking random demimortals about things like this."

"Modred. Come on. You've got to give me something."

He hails a cab. "You shall have a ride home. Anything more will have to wait. Just this once, you must promise not to be reckless."

"I'll consider it," I say, "if we can stop for curry fries."

7

I'm wired when I get home, although the curry fries have taken the edge off. Modred waits in the cab until he can see that I've opened the door. He has the dating instincts of a Teutonic Knight. I hear music from the hallway. I take off my shoes and walk barefoot into the living room. Lucian is on the couch, drinking a beer and listening to CBC Radio 2. He sees me and smiles.

"Hey. I got your text."

"What text?"

He hands me his phone. There's a text from me, sent two hours ago, which says: *brg 2 prngls sksi*.

"I must have sat on my phone."

"I thought you were saying, *Bring two pringles, sexy*.

So I brought both sour cream and barbecue. They're in the kitchen."

"Wow. Thank you. I just ate with Modred, but those are going to be bully when I wake up tomorrow and don't feel like cereal."

"Should I stay?"

I sit on his lap. "Yes."

He kisses me. "How was the party?"

I could be surprised, but at this point, it's a waste of effort. "You got wind of that tricky maneuver, did you?"

"Quartilla's parties are well-known. It's already all over Twitter that Modred showed up there with an OSI. Plus, I can tell that you touched a phasma."

This makes me hesitate. "Oh, really?"

"Yeah. Your breath's frosty." He draws me closer. "You think I can't tell that you're healing from an attack. I hear your bones mending. You don't have to tell me what happened. Just promise to be careful."

"You first."

"Did you learn anything from Quartilla? She's an aging hipster, but she knows a great deal."

"Lucian."

"What?"

I kiss him. "Was there a funeral?"

He looks at me strangely for a second. Then he touches my face. "Yes. Trinovantum is in mourning. The nightingales sing of nothing else."

"You must miss him."

"I do. He was a fair lord and a friend."

"I wish I could tell you something, but"—I arrange myself in his arms—"Selena tells me nothing. I'm caseless. I just follow vampires around and get hit on by spirits."

"I don't know much either. Deonara's doing her best, but it's not enough. Powers are shifting. I'd rather be in Vancouver at the moment."

"You love us for our foliage."

"Huh." He kisses me. "You're so right."

We stop talking. We take off our clothes and get under the blanket. Lang Lang plays Liszt on CBC 2. His body is beautiful because I can feel its thorns. He's like a flower doing its best on an asteroid, naked to so many cosmic terrors.

My phone lights up like a Christmas tree at three forty-five a.m.

It's Selena. I think the first word out of my mouth is "brush" for some reason. I blink and listen to her. What I've always loved about my boss is how she can talk about a crime scene as if it's nothing but a messy bedroom. She tells me that the Seneschal is dead. He was a very old bird. I expected him to die eventually, but not like this.

"Why do you need me there?" I ask.

"You'll have to come see for yourself. Bring Siegel and Sedgwick."

"They're not in my pocket, Selena. I can't just fetch them."

She's already ended the call.

I'm glad that Lucian went home earlier. I don't want to have to keep waking up beside him with shitty secrets. I think about the text that I saw on his phone, but only for a second. "Bro" is something guys say because they dislike the texture of words like "sweetheart" and "beloved." Maybe the text came from a necromancer school buddy. That would make him a necro-bro, which, now that I think about it, sounds offensive.

We take the van to Stanley Park. I can see flashes of light coming from inside the grotto of the Seneschal. The floor is made of hard-packed earth, so shoe covers don't seem necessary at this point. Becka photographs the walls. Her blue forelock glows in the dark. Linus sorts through an already-overflowing box of bindles, all labeled, sealed, and time-stamped. Cindée, who almost never leaves the lab, is talking to Selena while holding what looks like an ancient Dutch *haakbus*. The place has been completely ravished. All the Seneschal's beautiful and dangerous things lie scattered in piles on the ground, some broken, others angrily trying to get away. A clockwork duck walks around in circles, as if building up steam. As I watch in fascination, it shakes itself, then deposits a lump of metal close to my shoe.

I walk over to Selena and Cindée. "Where is the body?"

"In the bedroom," Selena says. "Cindée, put that down."

"It's got a lovely firing mechanism."

"It's old and loaded. Put it down."

"Fine."

Derrick raises his hand. "Question. Why is Tess here?"

"That's tricky," Selena says. "Follow me. Don't step on anything. He was a hoarder, and I've already learned once tonight that the little things are weirder and more dangerous than the big ones. Just be alert."

We go down a narrow hallway. A spider crawls across the wall, and I wonder if it's real or mechanical. There's a spinning box on the floor. I gingerly step around it. *Hellraiser* taught me that pointy boxes are just bad news. The bedroom is little more than a cell with a stone slab. When I see the body, I can't help but think of the legend of the phoenix, who gathers the kindling for her own pyre. What was once the Seneschal, an avian demon, is now a calcined nexus of bones and charred cloth. The smell is overwhelming. We pass around the Vicks bottle in silence.

"Is the stone actually burnt?" I ask finally.

"Oh, yes. It's melted in places." Selena turns to me. "The body isn't what I needed to show you. Look up."

"No. Not again—please let it just be the friendly giant this time."

"Just look up."

I do. My name is on the air, *Corday*, written in smoke.

It drifts around the uppermost part of the cavern like a dazed moth.

"Is that Polybius magic?"

"That's what it looks like."

"Then why didn't you call Lucian?" The words leave my mouth before I can stop them. I feel the need to come to the defense of my boyfriend, despite the fact that I know he doesn't actually work for us.

Selena gives me a look. "Necromancers aren't the only ones who know smoke magic. And I'm sure the Seventh Solium has enough fallout to deal with. Right now, what concerns me, Tess, is that your bloody name is hanging over us. Why would someone just leave your name here?"

"How should I know?" I feel myself growing defensive. "There are loads of Cordays in the BC Yellow Pages."

"That's pretty weak."

I sigh. "You're right. What does this mean, exactly?"

"It means that we'll need to interview both you and your mother."

"I hardly see what she has to do with this."

"Maybe nothing. But she's a Corday. She has to come in."

"This is ridiculous. More so than usual."

"You know," Miles says. "There might be a way to tell where the smoke magic came from. I can ask the room."

Derrick looks at him. "Maybe you've forgotten, but the last time that you queried a room like this, I had to rescue you from hungry materia vines."

Miles signs, *Thank you, dear.* Then he says: "Point taken. But that was a trap laid by the Iblis. I don't have such a bad feeling about this place."

"Try it," Selena says. "But take care."

Miles approaches the cremains of the Seneschal. His expression goes blank. I feel the dark air skip a beat, as if the room is clearing its throat. Then Miles begins talking with his hands. There are some hand shapes that I recognize, like "power" and "demise," but he's talking too fast for me to connect anything. He touches his hand lightly to his mouth, then repeats the sign, which means "speak." I watch my name turn lazily in the air above us. Maybe it's just a metaphysical text gone wrong. Or the message is meant for my mother. Neither possibility excites me.

He's silent for a few moments. What must a conference call with space feel like? I wonder. Stones usually just spit at you, unless you're fluent in their language. Miles turns back to us, looking a bit queasy. I guess that's my answer. Talking to space makes you carsick. He wipes his forehead, then says: "The room isn't making sense."

"Can you unpack that statement?" Selena asks.

"It contradicts itself. The space remembers fire and death. But it also remembers something being born. The Polybius magic was a part of neither. It came from somewhere else. The room says it doesn't belong here."

"Becka recorded it and took pictures," Selena says. "That's all we can do, since it won't survive transport. Even if it did, we have no tests for smoke."

* * *

Our house has become a fair. There are booths, tents, and a real Ferris wheel. I have to find everyone so I can ask them what magic is. First I get mini-doughnuts, holding the hot, sugary bag to my chest in place of a map. I find Derrick in the fortune-teller's tent. The fortune-teller is Mr. Corvid's head. Derrick shuffles the deck out of kindness. They both ignore me.

"What is magic?" I ask Mr. Corvid's head.

"A grindstone," he says. "It scrapes you away, until only what's sharp in you remains, until your iron grief is undressed."

I turn to Derrick. "What is magic?"

He keeps shuffling the cards. "An alphabet," he says. "A syllabary. Its conjugations are lightning, monsoons, and tectonic feuds."

I leave the tent feeling less sure of everything. I find Mia on the Ferris wheel, admiring its polish. Our small car rocks back and forth. I wish she would hold on to something, anything, but she has no fear.

"What is magic?" I ask her.

"A needle," she says. "It's terrible. It cuts, it snags us by our loops, it makes minced pizza out of us, and there's a lot of pain because it's hard to move when you're two-dimensional and stitched into an arras. But it also makes fruit, and foxes, and other important things."

I leave her circling on the Ferris wheel. I find Patrick

playing Skee-Ball. He hands me a Japanese body pillow, which he's won. Holding it, I ask: "What is magic?"

"It's like new pajamas. And Radiohead, I think."

I take the body pillow and walk to the haunted house. I find Miles crouched underneath a table, pretending to be a disembodied hand in a bowl full of uncooked spaghetti. He waves at me.

"What is magic?" I ask.

"It's several things," he replies. "But don't repeat them, okay? Hugging. Digging. Spelling. Sucking. Edging. Rimming. Meowing. Lying. Spitting. Presuming. Disinfecting. And Reverse Cowboy."

I leave him and walk to the petting zoo. Modred is having some sort of colloquy with a Shetland pony. He has an endless supply of apple slices.

"What is magic?" I ask him.

"The teeth that made me," he says, petting the animal lightly. "The sound of the mercy bringers in the morning, plunging their knives into whatever still moves."

I keep walking. I reach the outskirts of the fair. Lucian is in a dark corner, repairing a broken ride. I notice a Vorpal gauntlet among his tools. I should warn him about how dangerous they are. Instead, I ask my question: "What is magic?"

"A risk," he says. "Like living with dragons, or eating something that fell on the floor six seconds ago. Or pissing with the door open."

I keep walking, past the retired machinery, until I

reach the exit. My mother is waiting for me in the parking lot.

"What is magic?" I ask her.

"Don't be so literal," she says. "Just help me figure out where I parked."

I wake up early on the morning of my interroga-tion. I have no idea how I'm supposed to explain why someone wrote my name in smoke and then let it loose like a moth to flutter around the Seneschal's cave. I'm not sure I even want to know. I lie in bed for a few moments. The house is silent, except for the faint rustle of Derrick's delicate snores. I throw on some clothes and leave as quietly as possible. Well-dressed people are running to catch the SkyTrain, while the street punks and their dogs slowly rouse themselves. I grab coffee and a planet-sized muffin at JJ Bean. The barista wears a name tag that says, HELLO, MY NAME IS PHOENIX. The four-barrel roaster in the middle of the café smells like a dream. I thank Phoenix and walk to the station, where people are crashing into one another like players on *Logan's Run*. Luckily, being a long-term Vancouverite has taught me how to avoid the bite of umbrellas.

When I was a little girl, we used to spend our summers camping at Cultus Lake, in nearby Chilliwack. The cooler was always full of vegetables, pop, and deviled-egg sandwiches. My mother would sit in a folding chair, watching me as I leapt off the pier. She was convinced that you'd get cedar itch by swimming anywhere near Maple Bay, so we always went to Entrance, which was packed with sweating families. The sand was so hot that my toes felt like Tesla coils. I had no fear of older boys in swim trunks, although I did avoid the girls who were always whispering and eating ice cream. I trusted the water and the light that warmed it. I trusted that no matter how far out I swam, I would still remain beneath my mother's gaze.

Now I trust almost nothing. The SkyTrain rocks from side to side, and I keep quiet within my skeptical core. I used to trust magic, but it mostly just fucks me over, so I've put it on probation. I've given it a time-out.

This is my life now. Wake up; take transit to a place where I no longer work, as if searching for the shadow of my former job. Get ignored or patronized, like a child wandering through a museum. Get told not to touch anything, especially the sculptures. Get attacked for no reason. Then I go to sleep and it starts again. Is this really the vacation I was looking for? If so, I'm an idiot.

I walk to the CORE building and check in at the security desk. The guard swipes my ID and frowns. She swipes it again.

"What's wrong?" I ask.

"Your chip isn't working. Did you immerse the card in water?"

"No," I lie.

"I'll have to issue you a temporary card." She reaches under the desk and withdraws a new blank ID chip, which she inserts into her computer. "What part of the building are you visiting?"

I start to say, "Forensic unit," but then stop. The Forensic unit is a medium-security zone that any OSI can visit. My OSI-3 clearance gives me access to the entire unit and parts of the subbasement, but nothing below that.

"Inhuman Resources," I say.

The office of Inhuman Resources is located in a restricted section of the subbasement. I've never been there, but people are always complaining about it. Just getting through the door requires a unit director's clearance.

"Selena Ward is your supervisor, correct?"

"Yes." My mouth is dry.

"And you're a level three?"

"I'm due for a promotion soon."

The security guard frowns for a moment, staring at the screen. Then she types something and hands me the warm new ID card.

"All right. This will give you access to the blue sector of the subbasement. The IR office is door number 113. Stay away from doors twenty through twenty-eight. This clearance is only good for twenty-four hours."

"Got it. I'll try not to get trapped in a broom closet."

"Right." She looks oddly at me. "Have I seen you before at Sawbones?"

"That's possible."

"You know Lady Duessa."

"We're hardly Facebook friends, but yes, I do talk to her sometimes."

"What's she like?"

"Scary."

I pass through the second checkpoint and take the elevator to the subbasement. The moral part of my brain—Derrick's voice, basically—is screaming about how wrong this is. But my old teacher, Meredith Silver, used to tell me that I should never pass up the chance to learn something new about my world, even if it meant taking a risk. According to Selena, I'm practically retired, so I can't imagine how they'd even punish me for a security breach. I can always just say that I was visiting Esther in the data archive and took a wrong turn. Who knew that dropping my ID in the ocean could actually work out to my benefit?

I exit the elevator and follow the signs. Eventually, the walls turn from white to blue, so I assume that I'm going in the right direction. Doors twenty through twenty-eight have no identifying labels, but I can feel some pretty intense materia leaking through their reinforced steel. The security guard was probably right. As the numbers increase, the portals get weirder. OFFICE OF LOST TIME. OFFICE OF DEADLY FORCE. OFFICE OF CANTRIPS AND CLAUDICATIONS. Door eighty-three is marked simply: REFERENCE TEXTS. It seems innocuous, but someone has placed a strong sensory block on it, so I haven't the faintest idea what's actually on the other side. I suppose, in my line of work, noncirculating texts are far more dangerous than automatic weapons.

I'd always assumed that the CORE kept all of its information on data sticks and durable hard drives. It's weird to think they might actually keep monographs and oversized atlases, too. My curiosity gets the better of me. I swipe my card in the reader, and the door opens. I know that, somewhere in the building, a security program has recorded my entry. There's nothing I can do about it now. I walk in.

The room isn't what I suspected. Instead of a space filled with shelves, it's barely an alcove. There are no books, just a slick metal table and chair. I sit down, and realize that the table is actually a flat-screen console. A biometric program blinks patiently, waiting for my fingerprints. I lay my hand across the panel. I feel a light pinch. Then the table asks me what I'm looking for.

"Excuse me?"

"Welcome to the CORE Special Collections," the table repeats, speaking in Majel Barrett's voice. "Please enter a search term so that I can find what you're looking for."

"Okay." I think for a second. "Lord Nightingale?"

"Did you mean a small passerine bird?"

"No. Lord Nightingale of Trinovantum."

"Did you mean Nightingale Elementary in Vancouver?"

"*No*. What's wrong with you? *Lord Nightingale*."

"Did you mean the Canadian Nurses Annual Nightingale Gala?"

I sigh. "How about 'Ferid'?"

"There are two items that match your search criteria. One is a captured video file, and the other is a document. Which would you like to view?"

"The video."

An image appears on the surface of the computer. Patrick, Selena, and I are in the interrogation chamber. I realize that this footage was taken last year, when we first met Arcadia. I listen to her coldly answering my questions by speaking through the mouth of the Kentauros demon, Basuram, whom she would later kill.

"Let me see the document," I say.

A scanned PDF image appears. It seems to be a transcript of a conversation between my old homicidal boss, Marcus Tremblay, and an unknown subject. Parts of the transcript have been blacked out, but near the bottom, Marcus asks: "What demonic species do you belong to?" The subject replies: "We no longer have a name. We serve the Ferid, and that is all we have left. Our service."

According to the time stamp, this interview occurred in 1995, a full three years before Marcus allied with the vampire Sabine Delacroix and tried to kill me. When Selena first spoke with Arcadia, she'd assumed that the CORE had never had previous contact with the Ferid, who, as far as we could tell, were colonizers. It stood to reason that Marcus wouldn't tell anyone. He was always a dick.

"Search for Tessa Isobel Corday."

"There are three documents and one video."

"Let me see the video."

An image of my thirteen-year-old self appears. Meredith Silver is inducting me into the CORE. She asks me to raise my hand and repeat after her.

"In the name of every power and potentate," I say (through my braces), "I swear to uphold order and defy disintegration. I will keep positive relations with the materia of this world, and never enlist it for selfish means. I will never harm a normate, nor reveal myself or my occupation to their community. I will use my abilities to protect life, ease suffering, and seek justice for immortals who can no longer speak for themselves. This I swear, before every power and potentate, until the darkening of the ways."

Meredith takes my hand. "Very good. Now you are one of us, and this is a bond that cannot be broken, not even by death."

But it is breaking, Meredith. It's breaking every day, and I can't stop it, because I don't know what magic is anymore. I have to wander around a dream-fair, asking everyone I love, and their answers are weird and fucked and unsatisfying. You knew, Meredith. You gave me your athame, silver like your hair and sharp like your tongue. You always knew what you were doing, but I don't. What world is this, where a vampire can break your neck right in front of me? What world is this, where a girl like Mia is orphaned because she happened to be born like me, raw and vulnerable to those horrifying powers and potentates? To whom did I swear? What do they look like and where do they live? I know nothing about them, save for their genius, their hunger, and their remoteness, like infernal quasars. At least the Ferid reveal themselves to their servants. I don't know who I was indentured to. I don't know who or what reached an opaque hand across space, saying: *Awake, little girl, and be ours.*

"Would you like to search for something else?"

I stare at the black screen. "No," I say. "I'm tired, and I have an interrogation to get to. Thanks, though."

The computer turns itself off. I leave room eighty-three and head back to the elevator. There aren't enough search terms in the world to understand the CORE, and I don't have time to keep trying. I should have figured that out ages ago.

8

"State your name for the record."

"Tessa Isobel Corday. Can I have a cigarette?"

"No."

"That hardly seems fair."

"There's no smoking in the interrogation room. Just try to answer the questions as best you can. This shouldn't take too long."

"It would go a lot more smoothly if I had a cigarette."

"Tess."

"Fine. Sorry. I'm ready."

Selena glances at a folder on the table. Like most CORE folders, its precise contents are a mystery, but I know they're not good.

"When did you first encounter the avian demon known as the Seneschal? Describe the encounter."

"Two years ago. Lady Duessa hinted that he might know something about a suit of armor that belonged to Luis Ordeño. I gave him a shirt with a bedazzled kitten on it, and he traded me some information."

"Did you tell him anything about Ordeño's murder?"

"No."

"What did he tell you about the armor?"

"Nearly nothing that was comprehensible. But he did suggest that it had some connection to an old myth, about an alchemist and a Manticore. Which turned out to be true, if you remember."

"Of course." She looks again at the folder. "What about your second meeting? Walk me through it."

"I asked him some questions about an Aikon, which belonged to Ru's brother. At the time, we didn't know what it was, but he explained to me that it was an organ."

"Were you alone?"

"No. Mia was with me."

Selena frowns. "You took a minor to see a bird demon?"

"He was harmless, and I was trying to get her away from the vampire community center. Nothing happened. He even gave her a teakettle."

"What do you mean?"

"Exactly what I said. He gave her a brass teakettle as a present. It's sitting on the mantel in my living room. A bit beat-up, but still pretty."

"So—" She exhales. "You're saying that you allowed a demon to give a potentially dangerous artifact to a minor in your care."

"Oh, come on. It's not dangerous at all. You could pick up the same thing at any souvenir shop in Gastown."

"Was Mia Polanski with you the first time you visited the Seneschal?"

"No. Patrick came with me that time."

"Right." She scribbles something down, underlining it fiercely. "So you brought another one of your wards to visit. It sounds like you've been treating the Seneschal's cave like a bed-and-breakfast."

"They were fine. It was safer inside the cave than outside, in fact. It wasn't until we left that we got attacked by an insane necromancer. That was the first time. The second time, nothing untoward happened. It's not like I took them to Lees Trail. Both nights ended in soft-serve ice cream, not bloodshed."

"Fine. So, you and the Seneschal never spoke about anything other than the cases that you were investigating."

"No. He was a bird of few words."

"You're going to have to return that so-called kettle, you know."

"But it was a gift!"

"We'll have to analyze it."

"You mean break it into pieces and immerse it in weird solutions. No way. It's Mia's. He gave it to her."

"You're being unreasonable."

"What's unreasonable is wasting money to probe a kettle."

"Don't worry about the money. Just bring it to the lab. Most of the Seneschal's items were destroyed or damaged irreparably. What you call a kettle might be the only surviving artifact from his horde, and we need to have a look at it."

"Fine. Mia's going to freak, though. She loves polishing it."

Selena leans forward and steeples her fingers. If she were a Great White, this would be the equivalent of charging. "All right. We've compared video of the Polybius letters to other exemplars that we have on file. The lab has no experts on smoke magic, unfortunately, but we were able to subject it to handwriting analysis."

"And?"

"It's your writing, Tess."

I stare at her. "Get out of here."

"The directionality of the letters, the loops, the hesitations—they all accord with exemplars we have of your writing. The only difference is that the composition is shakier. This could be because of the medium, or because the text was written when you were younger. It more closely resembles samples of your writing that we collected when you were first admitted to the CORE."

"How many of these samples do you have?"

"How many forms have you filled out since you joined?"

I blink. "A lot."

"Tess, I can't think of a gentler way to say this. I don't know how, or why, but at some point—maybe years ago—you wrote your name in smoke and left it in the Seneschal's cave. The handwriting doesn't lie."

"I don't know the first thing about smoke magic."

"Maybe you did at one time."

"Selena—"

The door opens, and Derrick walks in. He looks uncomfortable. I give him a small wave.

"I think we're almost done," I say. "Then we can go for coffee."

"I—" Derrick swallows. "Tess, I'm not here to take you to lunch."

There's a catch in his voice. I look at him strangely. Then the reason for his presence hits me. I go cold. I turn to Selena.

"No way."

"I'm sorry," she says, "but it's the most efficient method of interrogation available to us. At this point, we need all the answers we can get."

"But why does it have to be Derrick?"

"I think you know why," she murmurs.

And I do. Even as the question leaves my mouth, I know exactly why he's been chosen for this job. I can't lie to him. Of all the telepaths in the world, he's the one most likely to carve through my defenses.

He sits down next to me. "I'm sorry," he whispers.

I can't look at him. "Just do it," I say. "Quickly."

Derrick puts his hand on mine. At first, I feel nothing but a tingle in my scalp. Then I feel heavy. The room darkens. I try to pretend that I'm at the dentist, but it doesn't work. He's my best friend, my rock, my *person*, and now he's sifting through my memories with draconian efficiency. I want to throw up. I close my eyes and let his power carry me forward, inch by inch, until the room is mostly gone, until my resistance melts and he can read me completely.

I see a little girl, about nine years old, sitting on a fur rug. Candles burn in stone alcoves, shedding multicolored wax. The Seneschal sits cross-legged on the floor next to her, preening his feathers.

"Again," he says mildly.

The little girl reaches out with her index finger. A nimbus of smoke collects around her small hand. Slowly, carefully, as if writing on a lined page, she traces her last name in seething calligraphy. *Corday*. It hangs on the air.

"Well-done!" The Senescal reaches out and snatches the autograph. Then he places it in a jar and seals the lid. "Should keep. Names tend to."

"Is it bad magic?" the girl asks.

He shakes his tail feathers. "Magic is not human. You, me, we can be good, can be bad, can be stupid—magic *is*. It reflects. Like fire, or cats, all depends on what direction you approach from."

"I think I understand."

"Sweet girl." He touches her face lightly. "Go find your mother."

The vision collapses. I'm back in the interrogation chamber. I'm sweating and pale. Derrick touches my hand. I recoil.

"Are you okay?" he asks.

I say nothing.

"What did you see?" Selena asks.

I stand. "Let him tell you. I'm going."

"Going where?"

"To find my mother."

"Tess, we've been calling her for days. Nobody knows where she is."

"It sounds like she's got the right idea."

"Tess—" Derrick tries to touch my shoulder.

I punch him.

It's the first time I've ever hit Derrick. The first time I've ever wanted to. He staggers back, pressing a hand to his cheek, which is reddening. His eyes are shocked. He opens his mouth to say something, but nothing comes out.

"You should have said no," I whisper. I'm so angry, I can barely get the words out. "You should have recused yourself, or said it was a conflict of interest. You should have found a way. But you didn't."

"I'm sorry," he says again. "I had no choice."

"There's always a choice, and you made yours."

"It's not that simple, Tess."

"It was. But it's not anymore."

I walk out of the interrogation chamber. I manage to get to the elevator and wait for the doors to close. Then I lean against the metal wall and cry, not just for Derrick's betrayal, or for Selena's apathy, or even for my mother's glorious deception. I cry, in the end, for the memory of a feather touching my cheek, and the tremulous voice of an old bird, assuring me that I am lovely and good.

I don't know where I'm going, which is nothing new. I let anger and momentum carry me down Burrard Street. I run into a protest, which has reached critical mass on the steps of the art gallery. People wearing Al-Awda T-shirts are yelling in a variety of languages about the Palestinian right of return. A girl raps in Arabic. Every tongue is charged with anger. I am an imbecile who knows nothing of this conflict, save for what I've read in *Drinking the Sea at Gaza*. I give myself up to the crowd. If I close my eyes, it's like a west coast version of *Beautiful Losers*, with everyone lifting their feathers to reveal their politics. Oh, F. Where were you when I was growing up magical next to the ocean? Where were you when I was dumb and horny and cruising Derrida at house parties, trying to fit in with the UBC brats? F, you delectable layabout, why did I never learn to be careless with my mustard or methodology?

Derrick's interrogation has shaken loose memories, which cascade like cherry blossoms and sinister maple leaves. I give my body to the axis of evil, primeval, and penultimate evil. I give my body to Vulcan's hammer; I bare my soft skin and my terrible curls to the witch hammer. *Folla, folla, fóllame Vulcan*, you bastard smith, you beautiful hunchback, you ancestor to Alexander Pope's metrical bitchiness. Your body *Quasimodo*, a double-dog-dare knot, impeccably tied and removed from view like the cold vetiver breasts of the *enana* Mari Bárbola. She wanted nothing but a pile of snow to cavort in. I should really learn to stratify my desires in this way. I should donate my organs to magic so that I can finally look my driver's license in the eye.

Derrick, what have you done? What have you uncovered? The curtains spread as the crowd pushes me toward the water. The only thing that bleeds worse than lost time is memory. I'm bleeding out. I'm a speck on a monstrous, flea-bitten narrative, an innocent shred of heme, a pink-eye rhyme. I exsanguinate, I dream, I make my way to the ocean with the rest of the bleeders. I understand for the first time that to recall is to be called violently when you're in the middle of something, like masturbating or taking a bath. To recall is to leap out of the water, to drop your hands, to open the door naked, dripping, and say: *What the hell are you doing here, memory?*

And memory breaks the chain on the door. Memory strides in, reeking of insult and ambergris. Memory sets fire to your afternoon. Bleeding out, burning, all you can do is ride the hyphen between now and then, a hyphen with no seat belts, no holy-shit handle, no brakes, a malicious wooden horse that drags you screaming through the ionosphere like Quijote on a bender.

My yellow bedroom. In photographs, the wallpaper has an unremarkable stencil but the carpet is steady-state and pleasant to the toes. I've arranged a scene in the royal chamber of Castle Grayskull. Evil-Lyn avoids the trapdoor and adjusts her headpiece. She and the sorceress have a colloquy. Drinks are served. My dresser always felt empty, but my bookshelf groaned. I would read anything. I would read for the sound it made. I would read under siege. I would read until I was dry. A numbered carpet and the press of others. We sing.

Four hugs a day, that's the minimum.

I said a-boom chicka rocka chicka rocka chick-a-boom.

I called the witch-doctor, he told me what to do, he said
ooh ee ooh ah ah
ching chang
walla walla bing bang

I told those little monkeys, no more jumping on the bed. I drew orcas and flying saucers. I murdered crafts. My letters were backward. I wanted more Munsch, less sunlight, one hug a day tops. I remember a walled-in play area, dark and aggressive. A boy nicknamed Oggie would flash anyone. I spent most of my time playing with three trees, which flatly refused to grant me ingress to Narnia.

I sit in the library, wiping snot on my sleeve. Fabric hurts me. I want to be quiet and nude. Two sisters pass by my table, snickering. They drop a tissue in front of me. Our lunchroom has ultramarine benches. You can buy ice-cream sandwiches, corn nuts, pizza subs kissed by the microwave. Chris Nixon deliberately wears tank tops. He stands outside of metal shop, indolent, pressing his ass against the cinder-block wall.

Sex for the first time is a matter of weights and measures. He's heavy and smells good, a star forward in love with the prettiest puck bunny.

Don't kiss me, he says. *I don't really know you. Don't touch my feet.*

Others follow. Who are you? Boys with crew cuts and secrets.

You are obsessed with Pavel Bure. You only read Russian moralist novels.

You want to rent porn after coffee. You force me to go off-roading. You steal my credit card and my tent. You lend me your mezuzah, which I mail back. You want to engineer the Borg in the UBC cybernetics lab. You refuse to discuss your philosophy paper. You think fondly of me while slicing deli meat. You demand your Banana Republic scarf back. You dance with me at the Odyssey and are flattered by the attention of boys.

You stand me up. You are stood up in turn. You introduce yourself with a paper heart and later give me a bacterial infection. You smoke pot with your grandmother. You speak endlessly of tow trucks and their drivers. You let me devour you after tea. You pay for both of my pineapple dogs. You say, *Look, don't tell anyone about this.* You say, *My parents are in town but I'll call.*

Forgive me for leaving you in the bathroom.

Forgive me for rejecting your vinyl billfold.

Forgive me for missing your recital.

You were all ahead of your time.

I smell seaweed. Unlike the little mermaid, I will hold out for something better and refuse to surrender my fins. The bleeding continues. Most likely, it's Ursula's magic. I know I said that I wouldn't sign the contract with the fishbone stylus, I know I said I would keep my voice, but everything looks different when you're drowning. Take the sound of my magic if you want, you tentacled hag. Give my guts to Flotsam and Jetsam. Only keep your promise. Throw both halves of me into a shrimper's net. Only keep your promise. Let me start over.

In sixth grade, for zoning reasons, I attend Robertson Annex. Every door is red. The bike rack has been licked clean. Every door is red except for one, which is green. That day I wear a skirt with white and green stripes. I'm pleasingly piebald, but resemble a candy cane. A boy with dark hair draws close to me. We stand on a ramp, which leads to our portable classroom. He says something nice and then hits me. My tears unnerve him. I'm angry and pinioned by shame. It's the first time a boy has ever touched me.

In the library, Miss Barth reads to us from *Hatchet*. The boys laugh when the pilot farts before dying. I'm intrigued by the computers. The catalogue is a system called Unicorn, which introduces me to *Ramona the Brave* and *Superfudge*. The halls beyond are dark, but the temperature in the library always stays the same. I wear shorts and a stained shirt that my mother has screen-printed with a duck's bottom. It reads: NOT PLAYING WITH A FULL DUCK.

A.D. Rundle Junior Secondary has something called Gummer Day. Students are flushed down toilets and up trees. I will dive into a toilet if it leads anywhere other than this place. There is one new development. Ninth-grade boys, wild hobgoblins in hypercolor T-shirts, cruelly calibrated to turn armpits electric purple. F is made class president. His sandy hair is a bowl that makes me want popcorn. Open my closet and you'll find colored scrunchy socks stacked like a pyramid of uncracked eggs, Mossimo jeans, a shirt with a pastoral scene from *Calvin and Hobbes*, a sandwich quietly giving way to entropy.

I hide in a blue bathroom stall. I dream. Three girls come in. I smell smoke and hair spray. I am Garion, Sendaria's favorite son. Mr. Wolf keeps an eye on me, while Aunt Pol disinfects my orbicular scar. The girls leave. I think about ways to escape tomorrow's PE class. Mrs. Covey thinks I am a waste of perfectly good atoms, and no longer trusts me when I claim to have cramps.

Rain sounds like applause on the deck. Pumpkins seethe in the garden. The cat snores with her claws in my hair. I push back my Princess Jasmine bedsheets and set fire to a pot of turkey soup. My deaf uncle walks up the stairs. He's drunk and wearing a padded vest. He smells faintly of fried cabbage.

Why have you got every light on in the house?

Because I'm twelve and the switches obey me.

Because it's dark, I say.

I try to look stunned, which I've learned makes people leave you alone. He goes back downstairs. I go into the master bedroom and steal the key to the hall closet, filled with 5-1/4 floppy discs and dirty magazines belonging to my stepdad. I analyze *Velvet*, a less scrupulous version of *Hustler*. Some of the women ride horses. One woman is trapped in a sinister garage. Occasionally, there are pictures of naked men, which make me anxious and curiously focused. I study each grainy ass and thigh with the intensity that, until now, I've summoned only for my rock tumbler.

I barely speak until we get our first computer. I make my needs known, but I'm not expository. Then my parents bring home a Tandy 1000 HX from Radio Shack. It demands disks like a tyrant, the amber light on the

3.5-inch drive always flashing. I use GW-BASIC to draw a medieval cityscape I saw in a fantasy book by Steve Jackson. I become obsessed with the CIRCLE command, which, when you add a time step, allows you to craft blooming white holes that eat the screen. We have trained our cat Sookie to use the toilet. I start to think of the bathroom as a shared litter box. We also have a collage room and a backyard smothered in wood chips. The grape vines enchant me. I turn them into a kind of desiccated parlor. Although I prefer the conditions of the den, I must pay respect to the caterpillars.

I trade a game that isn't mine with a sinister kid. One of the discs falls out of my knapsack. My stepfather finds it the next morning in a puddle. He throws it at my feet and goes to work. I resuscitate the disc with a blow-dryer, although the drive seems repulsed by it. I must conquer every game ever programmed by Sierra. I pore over hints that materialize only through the alchemical medium of cellophane. The cheat manuals remind me of my She-Ra sticker albums, with full-color representations of Swift Wind and Bow, effete leader of the rebels. I remove a glass pendant from our chandelier and use it to focus my latent telekinesis, which I feel is about to explode.

In *HeroQuest I*, your character must learn to climb. This can be done slowly, but I prefer to break my hero, physically and psychically. I position him in front of the tree by the healer's hut. *Climb tree,* I type, and all sixteen of his EGA colors wrinkle until he reaches the bough.

Climb down, I type. *Climb tree. Climb down. Climb tree.* He never complains. When he achieves proficiency, I reward us both by singing to Baba Yaga's house with chicken feet. *Hut of brown, now sit down.* If only real magic were that simple.

We're at the water now. I'm with Lucian. We lie in bed. Our fingers are proximal. On the TV, a bodiless pair of jeans is dancing. He snickers. I explore his waistband. We haven't hit naked yet, but I'm resourceful. My hand is having a great time. He smells like the midnight jungle of Perrin, which, by day, becomes a kaleidoscopic desert. I'm Bastian Balthazar Bux and he's my luck dragon. I'm delighted. I should have stolen this book a long time ago.

He dries me off gently. *There's nothing better,* he says, *than a freshly showered Tess.* In that moment, I believe him.

I'm walking through sand. I half expect to see him sitting on a log, doing whatever necromancers do diurnally. But he's not there. The crowd disperses. I watch the dogs of summer chasing tennis balls that zoom and flare like amber comets. One of them coughs on my foot. I take this as a sign and turn around, heading for home. My phone vibrates. It's Derrick. I ignore it and keep walking. He'll only be maudlin, and I can't deal with that. I need to find the one person who might actually have answers. But before that, I need a drink and some advice. I change direction and head for the Downtown East Side. If I'm fortunate, Lady Duessa will be receiving visitors.

9

Duessa's place is in full swing when I arrive. I can hear the music from the street. People have parked their track bikes, scooters, and skateboards everywhere. A vampire in plaid and Carhartt pants ushers me inside. He hasn't changed in the three years since I last saw him, save for the fact that he's wearing a Bluetooth earpiece. I nod politely and walk down the hall. There are deep grooves in the wood floor, made by soles more monstrous than mine. I reach the main room, which is alive with garlands and Christmas lights. Everyone is in their best drag, including the demons. A salad bar has been set up in one corner, complete with a soft-serve ice-cream dispenser, which I appreciate. I fill a paper plate with comestibles and look for somewhere to stand.

The music stops, and Duessa appears on a makeshift stage. Everyone applauds. Her strapless gown is trimmed with ermine. Her hair is extremely high, and she's wearing gold earrings made of tiny, pendulous amphorae that flash and tinkle as she walks. Her stilettos are actually stilettos.

She grabs the mic. "Good evening, ladies, boys, immortals, transfags, and gentlebitches. Welcome to my ball. Prizes will be awarded for best costume, best walk, and best weaponry. Start your engines and gird your loins, everyone. Our first category is realness."

The cheering soars. Duessa steps down and takes a seat at the judge's table, next to Wolfie, who is busy lighting votive candles with his index finger. The music resumes. A boy dressed as Cleopatra walks across the stage. Everyone holds up numbers. A girl follows him, wearing high-tops and a dozen pocket watches. Her score is decent. A youth in full armor is next. His hair is braided, and he's a bit older now, but I realize that it's Dukwan.

"*¡Guapo!*" Duessa yells. "Look at that fine Banjee boy!"

Dukwan smiles and gives his best walk. His score is high. A number of well-dressed hopefuls follow him. I finish my vegetables and move on to dessert, exhausting the chocolate sauce, which is swiftly replaced. I drift away from the festivities and down a hallway, eating my sundae. I pass the backstage dressing area, where vampire hairdressers and makeup artists work at lightning speed. The pile of discarded gowns resembles a beautiful Anglo-Saxon hoard.

I walk through a pair of stained-glass doors, which lead to a kind of study. Handwoven rugs are scattered across the floor. A giant astrolabe sleeps in the corner, while a winged orb flutters aimlessly above me. A desk made of carved rock crystal sits against the far wall. Votive candles burn atop it, throwing its quartz veins into startling relief. Books are stacked everywhere, some bound in leather and various hides, others barely held together by masking tape. I tell myself not to touch anything, not even the desk chair, which reclines.

"Do you have an appointment?"

The voice seems to come from nowhere. I scan the room. Then I look down and see a four-inch brass figurine staring up at me. She carries a tablet, which, I assume, must be Duessa's appointment book.

"Um—no. I don't. Sorry." I realize that she's a Lar—a household spirit. I've never seen one in person before.

"You really shouldn't be here, then."

"I was hoping to catch Lady Duessa after she's done judging."

"You and half the city."

"My name's Tess Corday. Maybe . . . I'm on a list somewhere?"

The Lar seems to relax, although it's difficult to tell, given that she's been sculpted from bronze. "Right. I've heard your name before. I suppose you can wait here. When she's done, I'll let her know that you've arrived."

"Thank you."

The figurine shrugs. "It's my job."

She makes her way swiftly out of the study, which still takes a few moments, owing to the fact that she has very short legs. I look away politely until I'm certain that she's gone. I don't know what I should do while I'm waiting. There's some kind of sideboard in one corner of the room, but I doubt that any of the bottles are drinkable. I finish my sundae and place the empty bowl on the counter, next to a red *cratera* covered in horny satyrs. My phone starts to vibrate. It's Mia calling, so I answer.

"I can't really talk. I'm in Lady Duessa's office."

"Whoa. What's it like?"

"Cool and creepy. Is everything okay?"

"Derrick says you won't talk to him."

I sigh. "That's between Derrick and me."

"Right. I'm sure you have a good reason. But in the meantime, your grown-up business is adversely affecting me."

"How?"

"Derrick refuses to make dinner."

"Oh, for—" I close my eyes. "Just heat up the leftover pasta."

"He bought all of the fixings for tacos, but he's too sad to make them. He just stares at the fridge. I think he was crying earlier. He looks super puffy."

"It's complicated. Just leave it."

"But I want tacos. We all want tacos."

"I have to go. I'll be home as soon as I can."

I hang up when she's in mid-moan. I realize that I may have to apologize to Derrick for hitting him. I don't want to, though. It's childish, but the anger keeps my wick lit, and somehow that's better than the desolation of knowing that my best friend invaded my mind.

I hear stilettos in the hallway. Lady Duessa enters the study. She waves at me and then collapses into the chair.

"Hey, sweetheart. Attia told me you were here. What's up?"

"I have a question for you. It's probably something I shouldn't ask."

"Those are the tastiest questions." She slides a box across the surface of the transparent desk. "Marzipan?"

"No, thank you."

"What's your question?"

"I need to know what Pharmakon is."

Duessa frowns. "Where did you hear about that?"

"A phasma told me."

"They're so fucking gossipy."

"So what is it?"

"Why do you need to know?"

"I got attacked by a vampire. He was tripping on something—really strong and bold enough to walk around during the day without catching fire. He acted like someone on PCP. I threw everything I had at him, and it was like he felt no pain. The phasma said it might have been something called Pharmakon."

Duessa looks me up and down. "Something's different about you."

"I'm on vacation. Don't I look well rested?"

"Not at all. There's something else."

"Oh. Well, I just found out that I knew smoke magic when I was a little girl, and that my mom used to hang with avian demons. That could be it. The whiff of my decomposing youth."

She laughs softly. "Figured that one out, did you?"

"Derrick ripped it out of my mind."

"Go easy on that boy. He's been through as much as you have."

"He's not the topic. Pharmakon is."

"*¡Calla!*" She shakes her head. "Easy with the word. Some words bite back, you know."

"Uh-huh. Is this going to turn into something with imagery?"

"Well, now that you mention it"—she stretches—"it does remind me of the time I was chilling at the thermae with the Dama de Elche. Crazy bitch had the most intense hair you've ever seen, and some badass necklace that she stole from a necropolis. But that's not the point. What you're asking about is straight-up dark, okay? As in, shit not to be trifled with. If it even exists."

"Can you just tell me what it is? Or should I ask the *de leche* lady?"

"De Elche. Doesn't anyone read anymore?" Duessa sighs. "All right. Pharmakon is made from undead leukocytes. You'd have to bleed a necromancer dry just to harvest a few drops. I don't know how to make it, so don't ask, but it's supposed to give whoever drinks it a kind of invulnerability. I guess if you were a vampire, you could use it like sunblock and it would make you stronger. You're sure the one who attacked you was tripping on something like that?"

"Not completely. But so far, it's my best lead. It seems like harvesting necromancers' white blood cells would be a pretty big treaty violation."

"When are you people going to learn that treaties are just paper? They mean nothing to immortals who are in the game."

"Then why do you keep signing them?"

She smiles. "It's a photo op."

"Of course."

She writes something down on a Post-it. She's just about to hand it to me, but stops. An odd expression crosses her face.

"I felt it," she says, "when the old bird died. Like a feather on my grave. He was an artificer, so whoever killed him must have been searching for something. If they're also mixed up in Pharmakon, you want to think twice before tangling with them. Got it?"

I eye the Post-it. "Yes. Understood."

She hands me the square of paper. "Go to this address.

Don't go alone. Bring backup. When they answer the door, ask for the cook. She's an expert on bad stuff like this."

"This is getting weirder by the second."

"Come here."

I approach the desk. She takes my hand and kisses it lightly. I feel a shadow of her power adhere to my skin. It tickles.

"That's my mark," she says. "It won't last for more than a day, but as long as you carry it, most of the cretins should leave you alone."

"Thank you."

"Don't go alone. I'm serious. Promise me."

"I promise."

She smiles. "Sweet girl. Seems like only yesterday, you had no idea what you were in the middle of, or where you came from. But you're learning now. Enjoy it. Learning is the hard part, but it only happens once."

"Is it supposed to feel this awful?"

She lets down her hair. "Oh, absolutely."

I doze on the bus. I dream about a feline heart, bloom of red muscle turning slowly in the dark. I can see the arabesque curves, silent transepts, secrets dropped carelessly in the left atrium that glimmer on the floor. I place a hand against the slick surface of the tricuspid valve, feel it clamp closed, then open. The heart doesn't know that it's dead yet, like a human heart it needs to be told. Music fills the dim chamber as the papillary muscle starts to pump, ever stubborn, doing what it knows how, the best that it can. Need reaches across the black spectrum and somewhere, in the dormant folds, a copper note sounds.

Departure is a trend. There are too many paths out of the body to be counted, too many exits, so hard to keep anything and not just locally. Humans leave in groups. They just pack up and leave; they dismantle, tents folding themselves, flattening into nylon absences. Animals, too. They grow dissatisfied.

It takes a lot to keep even one small life tied to a place. Warm textures of instinct pull them away, and they slip along wet concrete, along unearthly grass. Thick desire pulls them from their homes, from the foot of the bed, the old good spot by the fire. They know what they're doing, where they're going, no apologies.

One day we'll wake up and all of our pets will be gone, unable to cope with us any longer. And it won't stop there. Coffee will spray from cups, cursors will leap to their deaths from computer screens, music will trickle in streams of light from compact discs, emptying the sonic breath chambers onto all of the world's surfaces. When everything leaves, all we'll have left are surfaces—dark ice rinks and swimming pools choked with our leaves.

I think of Lucian. I remember the elastic silence of an old kiss. *I'm writing on your mouth—what am I saying?*

I laugh. *SOS. Send help.* I lift my head knowing a kiss is a narrative with the windows open, a space for theft, a scattering of grave goods. Things get in. You accept their incursion as a mirror accepts steam. *Send help. We may be sinking.* His fingers cool on the back of my neck. We're babysitting Baron, who watches us from the doorway, looking slightly embarrassed. Humans must seem so clumsy with their signs, honeypots cracked open with no subtlety whatsoever.

Can I stay on this bus forever? A man with gray hair nuzzles the neck of a woman in a leather jacket. She mumbles and turns away. Near the front a man has a garbage bag full of—what are they, buttons?—something that *clink*s when he moves. "Take me home," he says to the driver. "You know where I live; take me home." Can I stay on this bus forever? There would be no harm in being a balanced equation, skipping interstices like a rogue particle or a verb that has nothing to lose. Someone starts to sing "O Canada."

I blink from the wild glow of Save-On-Meats, Funky Winker Beans, all the souls gathered in front of the Carnegie Library.

"God look at them," a kid says.

The man with the garbage bag leans close to him. "You'll be one of them someday," he says.

The kid sputters, laughs, then stares moodily out the window.

I think of the cherry trees blading up like pink scandals in the air, backlit tender by light at Burrard Street Station. Magic lives there, circling the man-made fountains. Or maybe just the idea of magic, surviving on transit tickets, quarters, and cold puffed sentences stolen from backpackers in love, the braid of incidental words that from some angles could be warm braids of challah bread. If that magic were real, she would have to be made out of flowers and cooling cigarette embers, dark steel gleams and crinkles of foil, the brave hum of the trains as they carry us in bundles through unmapped space, the terrorism of our tunnels. The next station is never what you think.

She would prowl the edges of colonized thought, black paws against the rim of a white bathtub, skeptical, the way we test with one toe before sighing into hot water. Her voice would be rain on packed earth, an unlocking of ancient *arcónes*, or the stone kiss of smoke held in the lungs, held and kept, because the smoker is a lover who can't let go. Her questing wet nose in your face with its modesty. Her dandelion spells breaking over you. To live at all is to share a world with cagey magic, skeptical magic, asshole magic. But, honestly, the trees must belong to something; the blossoms that tongue each groove between buildings, the water and the stone and the serious man-made steel railings all must belong. This major artery where blood and starlight pump along the tracks, where banks and malls and office towers shudder and gestate in the concrete like baobab trees.

One time, the power went out in Lucian's loft. The heat stopped working and banged in the vents like a trapped animal kicking up dust. As a patina of coldness descended over everything, we lay on the rug eating brown bread right out of the package and letting it soak in bowls of steaming tomato soup, forming small lumped islands lost in continental drift. Afterward we huddled beneath his ugly striped afghan, thick with its odors of remembrance and transgression, bare feet cold and shocking each other. I could see under the table where a book had gotten lost or maybe buried; it was hard to say. Things do vanish into the intimate fissures of homes, into the coral reefs of beds with their quilts unrolled like someone's bare ankle, into the quietude of unmarked doors and spaces just wide enough for something to fly out. The gap between warmth and window, maybe love but just as maybe a blind rune.

It's quiet for a while, just the little hot pulse of Lucian's breath on my back, the drag of stubble. I think that maybe the heat will never come back on. We'll have to start a whole new civilization down here on the floor, in the space where the coffee table meets the rug, scraping stones together in the hopes that something will catch on fire. His fingers trace letters. I like to be written on but fear what that might mean. Lucian's inscription is laugh-heavy with vowels and sparse wooded silences, the settling of things in snow. Every attempt at translation leaves some crucial word out. I've lost the frontispiece, the illuminated letter that sets everything into motion. The colorful grotesques camped in the margins continue to baffle me.

When I was a kitten, I would sit beneath shifting panes of light through the open window and stare at my mother's books. There were so many, like bright toys or little rectangles of energy. We had an arrogant Persian with brown eyes that searched for unwilling laps. She exhibited a sun-kissed laziness as she sprawled on the stairway, not moving for hours, not even really watching the people as they stepped over her. One day the cat scratched me, leaving two half-moon puncture marks on my white knee. I drew back, startled, not understanding. Now I know that it was tender correspondence, that even the blood welling up from the wound contained a red, articulate love.

"Careful with the cat," she said. "They don't always play nice."

Actually, cats don't play at all; they live the most serious lives imaginable.

They have a lot to account for, a lot to manage. Ancient responsibilities whirl inside their pupils, inside the sad machines of their chain-linked thought. The agony of having to share this small slice of world with big breakable humans who are really just uncovered beating hearts walking around spilling their viscera and their words everywhere, not bothering to clean up. Animals are a smooth punctuation to human parataxis, resisting our love out of modesty. Sometimes I see Lucian's face with shocked cat's eyes looking at me, and where my body should be only a breaking kiss of shadow, and where my breath should be, only the feel of rough bark against an exposed tongue not ready for the touch.

Beyond the window, I watch the strays as they move sad and heavy along the streets, eyes glinting from Dumpsters, tails like satin pillows against the trash. I see the nomadic ones, dark prayer-flickers beneath the glowing signs in Mandarin. The girl with wet blond hair and, beneath her change cup, a cat asleep, head resting on scarred ankle. What complex trespasses does she dream of? What keeps her waking now and then to the sound of the trains as they thunder past, the clatter of souls, electric doors swinging in and out? She isn't heavy enough to make them open. She sits outside and watches the supermarket light, her expression difficult to read.

When we stray, we move upward through bark rings, through pools of curious black matter, to the edge of the outer rim of human kindness, where the only sound is our fallen pauses, which turn to shadows and fog in the early morning, the dignity of gutters, rain in all of its angles, where demons and felines move the spiral galaxies.

How many times have I run out of fatalism, out of the sense that my leaving would make something right? That from the *volta* of my body slanting away, some small tempered light would shine out? Now, my mother seems to have strayed, for reasons that only she understands. Her logic is painful but worthy. She never feared memory. Decay frightens neither of us. But as I stare out the window, something makes me hesitate. The breath on my back isn't Lucian's. I don't know where my mother has vanished to, and she has always been my GPS signal, my standard time.

"*Ronroneas,*" Lucian says. "I like it when you purr. *Preciosita.* My wise little hyphen." He claims an islet of my body and tends to it while I sleep, his tongue cleaning a problem of the flesh. We lie fused together and sepia beneath the dim, one myth, a cherubim rolling in the dark and tossing arms and tails about in a dreaming mess. A man's purring is the sound of every held kindness at the bottom of human roots floating up, silver lux against the prow of the body, a wind that cools the bones.

We purr only in private, not for just anyone. Heavy petting doesn't always work. Like cats, we sometimes need to be handled delicately. The hand must hover an inch above us, until we feel its warm currents and have to lean in. Bodies will turn toward each other in sleep. Men have been known to embrace this way quite by accident. Both Lucian's purr and Derrick's snore make me feel better about all things. I listen and close my eyes. World mending. To go back and hear that sound again. To return to my beloved crystal state. All mourning is a mourning for time travel.

The world hurts you. I realized this early. It hurts you because it can.

We hang over tenement buildings like strange clotheslines, our hearts about to drop—someone must catch them before they sing too far out.

Lucian, shadow, I look for you. In the discreet rustle of paws, the sighing of homeless cats as they burrow into stinking piles of cardboard, and the princely ones staring out from waterfront windows, peculiar in their sadness. Lucian, you aren't, you aren't, just null, no code, parentheses closing over. But are you safe? Are you somewhere guarded? Are you eating enough?

I look for you. In the graveyard where the white trains sleep like albino pups. In the puddles with their chorus of worms. In the drinking roots of the high black buildings, their windowed mouths closed to human plea, measuring starburn in cupfuls of lapidary. I look for you, in the words that our old Persian stepped over, the white square of page that her shadow fell across like an amethyst quill, shim shivering and brave enough, even if I barely noticed. Along untranslatable alleys, Dumpsters that hold sleeping roos in their pouch, kanga-like, long snakes of power line that fall across grooved footprints of space, I look for you.

Lucian. Through the cellar door, in rime and brine, I look, down all of the epic ways through which objects escape. I redact our papers and take out every name. I cut them out and hold them, brave little lines on foolscap. Lucian. Know this, at least. How carefully I peer. How long into the night's last watch I search for you. Count my mistakes as they wander by. Allow them their ministry. They care about you largely, about us. They like the feeling of doing what they have to do. As inevitabilities go, they're my personal best.

You've no idea—slipping away beneath the weight of our stupid, tired days—that I am saved by you, excavated. Take my hand knowing that I'm a beautiful mess. On my watch, some harm will come to you. Some doubt. Some pointless pain. But at least I carry a knife at all times. If I can walk once more with you through a painting and into the city of the dead, I promise to eat everything there, the fruit spread with its square black watermelons, the cold-cut trays, the scalloped potatoes, the glowworms, everything, even the air, even the verb. My body is all staircases, but it's yours.

I push open the doors and walk to Yaletown. The patios are alive. Everyone drinks Technicolor cocktails. This whole area used to be filled with dock equipment and factories, and now all that gets made here are people's reputations. Little dogs wait patiently, tethered to wicker chairs. The smell of global cuisine leaves me craving something bland, like dry toast or oatmeal. I may just have both before bed.

I ring Lucian's bell. One night, I know, he's not going to answer. I'll show up and there won't even be a note, just bare concrete floors. Like death itself, necromancers know when it's time to move. At any moment, he could step sideways into a painting and vanish forever. But tonight, he answers the door. He's wearing a housecoat and slippers. He smiles broadly when he sees me. I kiss him. I put everything that I have into it. When I pull away, he looks surprised, but happy.

"Can I come in?" I ask.

"After that entrance? How could I say no?"

"I need your help. And I need a drink."

"There's beer in the fridge, and I can warm you up some leftovers. How do you feel about Sky Dragon?"

"I love it."

"Then come in."

· IO · ·

We talk until we're delirious, until dawn bakes the
windows. I tell him about the vampire who turned to
water in my hands, about the Pharmakon—sorry,
Modred—about my trip to the CORE reference library,
which resulted in nada. We move in little pilgrim-
ages, from the couch to the bed to the floor. We drink gin
and devour salt-and-vinegar chips. He talks about Madrid
before the dictatorship, about the Retiro pierced by sunlight and his wonder at seeing traffic lights for the first
time, how he would watch them in silent awe. He tells
me that when his *abuela* first saw the army of cars circling the Plaza de Cibeles, she couldn't believe that each
of them belonged to a single person. I tell him about my

only friend when I was a girl, Eve, whose house burned down around me.

We lie propped on pillows, seminude and covered in chip detritus. We've switched from gin to ginger ale. I burn off my hangover using thermal materia, which I don't recommend unless you know what you're doing. Lucian makes a pearl of black flame in his hand. It's cold to the touch. I translate the monologue of the concrete floor, which mostly involves complaints about our shoes. He promises to go barefoot more often, which I think is sensible.

"So you've completely forgotten how to write in smoke," he says.

"I guess the knowledge is there somewhere. Derrick pulled it out of my mind, after all. But I can't touch it anymore. It was only visible for a second."

"Don't be too hard on him."

"Geez, that's what Duessa said. Why is everyone rushing to defend the telepath who broke into my head?"

"Because he probably had no choice."

"Look—" I shift position on the pillows. "I realize that I can be a monster sometimes. I'm not always the sunniest person to be around. But I would never invade the mind of my best friend."

"Right. And you've never used materia on any of us."

"Define using it *on* you."

"To protect us from an attack."

"That's completely different."

"Is it? Derrick and Selena were trying to help you by figuring out what your connection is to the Seneschal. And if they can learn something about his killer, isn't that worth prowling through your memories?"

"I'm not sure I like where this is going."

Lucian crawls over to where I'm sitting. He puts his head in my lap. It's impossible to resent him from this angle. I touch his hair. It's soft, like how I imagine a black swan's underbelly would feel.

"You have to forgive people," he says. "They often do stupid things when they think it serves a purpose. They trespass. They're careless with the breakable parts of you. But they mean well."

"People usually shine when given the opportunity," I murmur. "That's something that Derrick said once."

"See? Gay Yoda is wise."

I snort. "I'm absolutely telling him you said that."

"By all means."

"Lucian?"

"*¿Sí, corazón?*"

"Tell me about your brother."

He's silent for a beat. Then he puts his hand on my bare ankle. His thumb describes slow revolutions, as if etching something. "My brother is tricky."

"Okay. I can appreciate tricky."

He sighs. "We were always together. My hand was always in his. One day we went to Casa de Campo. This was before you could ride the *teleférico* across the river.

We were hiding from each other. Lorenzo hid so well that I couldn't find him. We were separated. I was so young. I remember that the trees seemed like giants. I remember how hot the sun was. I felt feverish. I saw something, like a shadow, or smoke. Black and violet. A bee stung my neck, and I fell asleep. When I woke up, I could hear my mother calling my name. She held me so tight. Lorenzo was crying. He kept saying how sorry he was. I told him that nothing happened. A bee stung me, and that was all."

I touch the lily tattoo. "It was the Iblis."

"I guess it was. I don't know what it did, exactly. But I realized that only Lorenzo could see the mark. He was scared of it. After that day, I heard shadows. I saw phasmas and pieces of lost people. And when our parents took us to the Museo del Prado, some of the paintings spoke to me. I saw past their oils and tinctures. I saw a city where death was king. Trinovantum."

"You must have been scared."

"Not at all. It was like seeing a beautiful animal. I was too young to realize that it had teeth. I wanted to touch it."

"How old were you when you first visited the city?"

"Seven, I think. At least, that's the first time I remember. I fell through a portrait of an infanta. I was staring at her dress. It was so big, it looked like she was carrying an enormous shell. My neck started to itch. Then I was in the gardens of Trinovantum, surrounded by night birds and cats. The House of Lilies took me in. They became my second family."

He gets up and goes to make coffee. I don't know if it's a feint, or if he's just caffeine deprived, but I approve of the gesture. Derrick convinced him to buy an espresso machine last year. It's candy red and perches like a bird-of-paradise on his granite countertop. He makes us both strong *café con leche*. Then he sits back down on our makeshift divan of pillows.

He stares into his cup. "I was always telling Lorenzo stories. How Lord Nightingale taught me to speak glow-worm. How I fed crab apples to nightmares and ducked beneath the questing legs of spider-demons. *Take me with you,* he'd say. But I knew it would be too dangerous. Then one day, when we were both teenagers, Lorenzo got into a fight with Papa. *I'm running away,* he said. I was scared for him. I didn't want to lose him to some American city. So—" His voice trembles slightly. "So I showed him the way."

He starts to cry softly. I've never heard him cry before. "I told him—*don't eat anything.* I told him again and again. But he wouldn't listen. I turned around for one second, and there he was, biting into a fig. *It's so good,* he said. *It's the best thing I've ever tasted.* And then—his whole face changed. I grabbed his hand, but it was already cold. He felt it. He knew. He could never leave."

I hold him until he stops shaking. I kiss him. *"Cariño,"* I whisper, "it wasn't your fault. You can't stop curiosity."

"I should never have shown him the way."

"You were both young. You would have told him sooner or later. You can't hide anything from family."

"I should have tried harder." He's regained his composure. He's no longer naked to grief. But I still hold him.

"Does this mean," I ask, "that Lorenzo is alive?"

"I know I said he was dead. But he is. He died that day. I had to tell my parents—" He shakes his head. "I lied to my mother. I told her that Lorenzo ran away. I forged postcards from European cities. But it was useless. All of the light went out of their lives when he disappeared."

"Is he still in Trinovantum?"

"He can't pass over like I can. I mean, it's possible, but he's like a ghost. I hardly ever see him. I don't think he ever forgave me for what I did. He doesn't want to talk to me."

"He was the one who ate the fruit. You did nothing wrong."

"I should never have shown him the way," he repeats.

I think about the message that I saw on his phone. I almost say something, but after all that he's just told me, it seems cruel to press. Maybe ghosts can send text messages. It wouldn't be the weirdest thing I've ever heard of.

"Does he, like—" I make a pointless gesture. "Does he have an address? Are there addresses in Trinovantum?"

"He wanders," Lucian says. "Sometimes Lord Nightingale would see him, and he'd let me know. But now she's gone, and I doubt that Lorenzo cares enough to check in with Deonara Velasco. The city is in shambles. They're trying to pull me back, to give me some new title with new responsibility, but there's nothing in that place for me anymore. My life is here. With you."

I kiss him. "I'm happy to hear that. But I'm not sure it's that easy to forget the place where you grew up."

"I grew up in Toronto."

"The place where you really grew up."

"Yeah. I guess."

"I think I have to go there."

He stares at me. "Have you not heard anything that I've just said?"

"Of course. I'm glad that you're telling me this finally. And I understand that Trinovantum is a scary place. But whoever killed Lord Nightingale—Theresa—is probably the same person who killed the Seneschal. In a situation like this, the CORE doesn't know their ass from a hole in the ground. They aren't going to go knocking on doors in the city of necromancers."

"And you don't work for them anymore."

"I still work for them. I'm just on vacation."

"Tess."

I take his hand. "I need you to come with me to visit this person that Duessa calls the cook. I have a feeling that these killings have something to do with Pharmakon. Isn't it always about drugs and money?"

"In your line of work, it's more often about souls."

"Souls are just another form of currency, and I don't say this to many people, but mine belongs to you. I'm making a deposit. One soul. Please keep it safe, because it's all I've got."

He touches my face. "You're trying to seduce me with metaphors, and it's working like gangbusters."

"Come with me," I say. "If this thing is killing necromancers, then you're involved whether you like it or not. Come be my muscle and my conscience. Then take me to Trinovantum. I need to talk to the new Lord Nightingale."

"It's a terrible idea."

"I know. But some small part of you agrees with me."

"I'm so bad at saying no to you."

"I realize that. And I appreciate it."

"Selena's going to—"

"Kick my ass, yell at me, call me a child, and threaten to cancel my pension. The usual dance. That's just how we talk."

"And Derrick?"

"What about Derrick?"

He stares at me levelly.

"Fine. I'll talk to him."

"Today. Promise."

"I promise to make up with Derrick."

"Because he loves you beyond all reason. As do I."

"You boys. How did I get so lucky?"

"You've got a horseshoe up your ass."

"That's a pretty way to put it."

He shrugs. "I can't help being pretty."

We get up. We do the dishes. We go through our ablutions. He soaps my back. I drag a cloth behind his ears until they're squeaky clean. I argue with my hair while he shaves, and I say nothing about the small Chia Pet that he leaves behind in the sink. I just wait for him to leave and then wash it away. I send a text to Derrick. *I love you and we can talk later today.* It's not an apology, but I'm still unsure whether I owe him one or not. If anything, I owe Miles an apology for denting his boyfriend.

I should sleep more, but the frayed ends of my consciousness feel good, like worn-in jeans. There will always be more coffee. There will always be a surplus of devotion and protection, because that's what families do. And there will always be broken rules and bloody knees, because that's what life does when you're busy painting definitions. I get dressed and come down the stairs. Lucian hands me a travel mug. He loves me like a lion. I take his offering and his hand. Together, we walk outside, blinking in the sunlight, like two clay figures recently given life. Full of vinegar and godsbreath.

"Lucian?"

"Yes?"

"Is your brother a ghost plant?"

He looks at me funny as we cross Broadway. "You mean, like, one of the skeletal flowers in the conclusus?"

"No. I mean, you told me once that necromancers were

kind of like plants. If your brother is trapped in Trino-vantum, does that make him more of a plant than you are?"

"We're not actually plants. We don't need fertilizer."

"I get that. But your explanation was a little fuzzy."

"I guarantee that the more you know about necromancers and their peculiarities, the less you'll understand."

"Granted. But—is Lorenzo more of a perennial?"

He sighs. "Okay. We're more like plants than humans because plants have more base pairs of DNA, but they're empty. Well, not empty, but . . . uncreated. If that makes any sense. Like flowers, we're full of empty drawers, and our power comes from all those little voids."

"You sound like a cheap koan."

He kisses me on the cheek. "Too bad. That's all you're getting. Besides. We're here." He surveys the restaurant. "Huh. I can see what Duessa was talking about. This place is a front if I've ever seen one."

The restaurant has no name, just a picture of a cow, which I assume means that they sell steaks. I can see through the dirty windows that every table is vacant. Like the inside of a necromancer. I'm not really sure how to accept the fact that my boyfriend has empty drawers inside of him, but whatever. I'm no proper judge of someone else's base pairs.

We walk in. The lighting is dim and, for some reason, Shakira is playing on the radio. *Lo hecho está hecho,* she growls. What's done is done. There's a huge bar with nobody to tend it, and the menus are dusty. After a few minutes, a waiter emerges from the back. He's a ghoul. His makeup is pretty good, but I can still see the decomposition. When you're undead, you really can't skimp on cosmetics. "Go MAC or go home" is the motto of most zombies.

The waiter stares at us without saying anything. I feel like we're trapped in a semiotic standoff. Then Lucian clears his throat.

"We need to see the cook," he says.

"She's busy."

"Lady Duessa sent us," I supply.

The ghoul rolls his eyes. "I doubt it."

"Oh, yeah? Come smell me."

Lucian gives me a look, but says nothing. The ghoul approaches me. He inhales cautiously, then nods.

"You're right. Her mark is on you."

"Told you."

"Fine." He points to a door in the far wall. "Kitchen is that way."

We go through the door and down a hallway that reeks of past meals and combination plates.

"Is that how you roll now?" Lucian asks. "Just asking random people to smell you? It seems like a funny way to establish credentials."

"The guy with plant DNA thinks I'm weird?"

"Geez. Don't be such a hater."

We enter the kitchen. It's really half kitchen and half crack den. Various illicit substances are bubbling and baking in pots. A giant squid wearing an apron stirs the pots with each of her arms. I realize now what the waiter meant. She's holding a cleaver. She fixes one luminous eye on us and shrieks something that sounds like profanity in all vowels. Then she spits ink at our feet.

I take a step back. "Do you speak cephalopod?" I whisper.

Lucian shakes his head.

"Great. That's just great." I wave at the squid. "Hello. Lady Duessa sent us. We have a question to ask you."

The squid waves her cleaver at us. We take another step back. I decide to try a new tactic. I point to the nearest pot.

"That smells awfully good," I say. "What is it?"

Her luminous eyes narrow, as if considering the sincerity of my question. Then she says, in a very thick marine accent: "Methamphetamine."

"Oh. How nice. May I take a closer look?"

She beckons me over with one tentacle—not the one holding the cleaver, to my relief. I walk over to the pot. The liquid inside it smells absolutely terrible, but I pretend that it's apple cider and smile expansively.

"Mmm. I'll bet it's quite delicious."

"It would not be my first choice," she mutters slowly. "But plenty of others seem to like it."

"I detect a hint of paint thinner. Maybe that's what gives it such a lovely bouquet. Did you think of adding that yourself?"

"I follow a recipe," she says. But I detect a hint of pride in her voice. I'm obviously going in the right direction.

"I have a question for you about another type of dish. It's a bit more complicated, but I can tell that you're an expert."

"Go on," she says. She's still holding the cleaver, but it's at half-mast now, which is probably the most I can expect from a wary squid.

"I heard that you might know something about Pharmakon."

Her eyes narrow. "Who told you this?"

"The Lady Duessa. She said that you were the squid to talk to about all things drug-related. She couldn't stop singing your praises."

The cook considers this for a moment. Then she says: "I do not think you could afford it."

"Oh, it's not for me." I gesture to Lucian. "He's rich, and he wants to contact your supplier. Unfortunately, he's also mute. Poor thing. He carries this little pad of paper around with him everywhere. It's kind of adorable."

Lucian glares at me, but says nothing.

Given that he's wearing cargo shorts, I'm hoping she won't draw the conclusion that he's also a necromancer. Can a squid smell that kind of thing? Can a squid smell at all? I'll have to remember to look that up later.

"I have not met him," she says. "He pages, and the waiter picks it up. Always a different address. *Albert!*"

The ghoul walks into the kitchen. "Stop screaming."

She gestures at us with one of her tentacles. "These two want to buy from the strange one. Are you picking up tonight?"

"Yes. But he said to come alone."

I point to Lucian. "He literally has money coming out of his ass. We could just wait in the car while you talk to him."

"I have a bike," the ghoul says flatly. "And I never talk to him. I just pick up the package from the mailbox."

"Fine. Let us come with you, and we'll leave some money and a nice note in the mailbox. We'll even pay you a retainer."

He frowns. "What's that?"

"Fifty bucks." I turn to Lucian. "Give the ghoul fifty bucks."

The waiter's eyes widen. "How did you know?"

"Your cheek is decomposing."

"Oh, shit."

Lucian gives me a look that speaks volumes. Extremely pissed-off volumes. Then he reaches into his billfold and pulls out a fifty. I knew it. He always carries an emergency bribe. Grudgingly, he gives the money to the ghoul, who pockets it.

"Fine," he says. "Meet me back here at seven thirty, and I'll take you there. You have to stay out of sight, though. He's crazy."

"I thought you said you never talked to him."

"I've seen him, though. I know crazy when I see it."

The sentiment seems odd coming from an undead creature, but considering the fact that I just grifted him, I can't judge. The truth is that this was a lot easier than I thought it would be. Which makes me nervous.

"We really appreciate it," I say. "We'll come back."

"Don't tell anyone."

"Of course not."

I extend my hand to the squid. "It was very nice to meet you."

She offers me one of her tentacles. It's rubbery and cold. I'm not sure if I should squeeze or not, so I just shake it slightly. Then Lucian and I leave.

Once we're outside, he glares at me again. "Mute? Really?"

"Think about it," I say. "If anyone asks, they're both going to remember a mute entrepreneur and some girl. That sounds nothing like us."

"Why couldn't you be the mute one?"

"Because you're too sweet and charming. I'm far more believable as a small-time drug addict."

"You scare me sometimes."

"In a good way?"

"In just about every way."

I smile. "I'll take it."

"What are we going to do until seven thirty?"

"I should probably talk to Derrick. If you want to be extremely useful, you can chat with Modred and see if he's learned anything."

"You're sending a necromancer to talk to a vampire. You must have an odd sense of political correctness."

"Modred doesn't really take me seriously. But if he knows that you're involved, he might let something slip."

"Involved in your unsanctioned investigation, you mean."

"Yes. Exactly that."

"Are you sure you know how to play this game?"

"I'm sure that you'll bail me out in the end. That's almost as good."

He takes my hand. "I'm not kidding. You don't have the CORE behind you this time. You're on your own. Please be careful."

"I never am. But thanks." I kiss him. "See you later tonight."

II

I come home feeling as if I've used up all my good words. It's just as well, because Derrick is asleep on the couch, slumped over Miles like a beautiful marionette. Both of them are snoring. Miles has one hand on the clicker, the other on Derrick's chest. My boys. They sound like dueling banjos. I wonder what they're dreaming about. Secret things that only queer boys understand, like Tori Amos liner notes, or the language of scarves. Considering that Derrick can read thoughts, I find it incredible that he's managed to fall in love. Maybe Miles thinks only proper things. Maybe he has the mind of a unicorn. He certainly knows how to be dirty in ASL, though. Maybe the thought isn't really what counts, but rather, the voice, the hand, the look. Thoughts come cheap, but when someone puts their hand on your back, gently, to guide you into a room, that matters. These small, moth-like gestures that form the geometry of care.

I sit down at the kitchen table to write Derrick a note. In my head, the note is hundreds of pages long and full of superlatives. I choose brevity. *Derrick. I love you, and I'm sorry I hit you. I'll be home later tonight. Don't forget that we need paper towels and vegetable thins.*

I add a semi-hysterical PS for Mia. *Text me when you get home.* I could keep going forever: *text me when you get to Berkeley, when you sleep with a boy/girl for the first time, if the power goes out, when you graduate, when you're sad or scared, if you need sweaters, when you get your heart broken, text me and I'll cross any surface to get to you.* But I can settle for knowing where she is tonight. Letting go is a work in progress.

It's hot outside. I find a patio and order a beer. It mixes with the coffee already in my stomach, and the two embark on a power struggle. I watch the Rollerbladers, the dog walkers, and the street punks blowing smoke. When I was little, I was an angry kitten, full of smoke and savage power. When I was little, a bird demon watched over me, and now he's dead. All of my teachers die or disappear. Is it me? Am I radioactive? Am I a poisoned well?

I stare at my fingers. If I concentrated, if I parted the atomic curtain and reached in, if I tugged just a little on the margins of the world, I could set this patio on fire.

But the truth is that I've always hated fire. I chose the earth, not just because stones asked me the time of day, but because the earth seemed like a book I was willing to read. The earth was something I could crawl into. I could be a blind worm digging, a submerged root, a sealed bulb with no intention of breaking the surface. I trust the earth, but not the other elements. They whisper behind my back like popular girls.

I was born with spines. I was born with opinions and occult specialties. I was born out of demonic wedlock. I was born out of mercy. My mother felt the alien plasmids in her blood, the foreign DNA, and instead of eradicating them, she said: *I call truce.* She injected a drug that solved everything. And here I am. It's the same thing that we did to Mia. *Here, take this shot, and you get to be human.* But origins can't be quiet. They clamor for attention, a litter of oracular piglets eating everything in sight.

What does it mean to be a demon's daughter? Should I be living in another world? Should I be getting more discounts? My father is a false rib that I've always felt but never known. Every day, I get closer to breaking through my chest plate and exhuming him, destroying him into consciousness. My mother must have realized this, and that's why she's disappeared. My beautiful mother, who, like Frigga, would protect me from anything with thorns if she could. But she forgot about the mistletoe.

I joined the CORE because it seemed to offer a way out, a solution to the daily feeling of being misunderstood, ignored, feared. The fire that consumed Eve taunted me from one direction, while the CORE beckoned me from another. But who was it who watched me from the sidelines? Was it you? Were you what I saw, in spite of the wind? You might have been a siren or a house on fire; I couldn't tell. I was always nearsighted. And so, I chose the CORE.

But I know nothing about them, this coven, this company. They block my questions at every turn. They give me things to do, cases to occupy my time, junctions to puzzle over, but never a real answer. I'm tired of agnosis. I've had enough of their protection. I need to expose their roots. Doing this, I realize, will not end well. But it will end. Love may be circular, but knowing is ending. I pay the bill and step onto the street. I've made my decision. I'm going to sin against those who offered me shelter. I have no other choice. Selena was wrong about retirement. I can't walk away from the CORE until I've seen its face. At least then I'll know what's hunting me. I'll recognize its scent.

I go to the Forensics unit. Everyone moves crisply beneath the industrial air-conditioning. My body feels frozen into relief. All my sins and freckles show. I linger in a peripheral hallway until two thirty, when I know that Selena will take a fifteen-minute coffee break. Then I make my way to Ru's place. Like a political prisoner trapped forever between time zones, Ru lives in this suite, dreaming of his home world and its beautiful methane storms. When I come in, he's listening to a CNN podcast.

He takes out the earbuds, pausing to disentangle the cord from his left horn, then smiles at me.

"Tess. I am glad to see you. This day has been highly unproductive so far. Would you like to give me five and accompany me to the music library?"

"You mean take five," I say. " 'Give me five' is a high five."

"Nothing that you just said made sense."

I extend my palm. "See? We've both got five fingers—"

"Actually, I have talons."

"Just slap my hand. That's what 'giving five' is all about. You give me your five fingers, and I give you mine. It's a greeting."

He slaps my palm uncertainly. "How was my gift?"

"It was great. Look, I need your help with something. Do you feel like going to the basement?"

He brightens. "There could be rats."

"Excellent. You can brush up on your colloquial rodent."

We leave the suite. The security camera records our exit. I'm not concerned, since people stopped checking the tape a while ago. There's only so much trouble that a Ptah'li child can get into, even in this building. We take the elevator to the subbasement. Ru studies the blue walls in fascination. I use my card to open the door to the reference library.

"What is this place?" Ru asks.

"It's an archive. How would you feel about messing

around with the computer? Selena tells me that you've reprogrammed the Nerve before, so this operating system shouldn't give you any trouble."

"Does it require an upgrade?"

"Not exactly. Watch." I activate the tabletop computer. "Give me information on Lord Nightingale," I say.

Majel Barrett's voice returns. "Did you mean 'Ode to a Nightingale'?"

"No. Lord Nightingale."

"Did you mean Florence Nightingale?"

I turn to Ru. "This is the only search term that stumps the computer. Is there anything you can do to loosen its tongue?"

The look that Ru gives me is not odd, but simply curious. "Are you asking me to override the machine's security protocol?"

"It sounds so break-and-entry when you say it like that. But yes."

He studies the screen for a few moments. Then he opens the keyboard interface and begins typing. His fingers are a blur. Every once in a while, the computer starts to say something, as if protesting, but he cuts it off with another stroke. Finally, it emits a tone, almost like an old 2400 bps modem scrabbling to connect to another line. I hear static. Then silence. Ru looks up.

"Ask it again," he says.

"Give me information on Lord Nightingale," I repeat.

The computer is silent for a few seconds. I wonder if

we've broken it. Then the voice returns. But it doesn't say anything that I can understand:

Non me tanqas, ya habibi
Fincad y en esu
Al-gilala rajisa
Bastate, ou fermosu.

I look at Ru. "Is this another glitch?"

"This is the sector that was encrypted."

I ask about Lord Nightingale again. The voice repeats its message. It's obviously a poem, but in what language?

"Fermosu," I murmur. "It kinds of sounds like *hermoso*, which means 'handsome' in Spanish. The rest sounds Arabic."

"I do not understand the dialect."

I look in my purse for a pen and paper. All I can find is a pencil and an old phone bill. I tear off part of it and write down the words.

"Tess. I have a question."

"Shoot."

He spits green acid on the far wall. The metal bubbles and melts. I realize that idioms can be dangerous when used carelessly.

"I meant," I say, "ask me your question."

"Oh." He looks slightly embarrassed. "Why do you think someone would go to such trouble to encrypt a poem?"

"It looks to me like a game of hide-and-seek. Someone made sure that this reference computer held no information about Lord Nightingale. However, they did leave a small piece of data in exchange, like a bread crumb."

"Will it lead to fowls?"

"Danger and disarticulation, most likely."

"But you are going to follow it."

"Yeah. I'm dumb like Gretel that way."

When I get to Lucian's place, Modred is there. The two of them are sharing a pot of tea. It would be normal, except that Modred doesn't actually swallow anything. He savors it in his mouth for a moment, then deposits it politely in a spit cup. This does not look like gathering information. It looks like a darker version of *As Time Goes By*.

"Tess." Modred isn't pleased. "I see you've spoken with Lucian about what transpired at Quartilla's party."

"It's not like we were making a lot of headway on our own. I thought involving another brain would help."

"You're only making things more complicated."

"We've been cruising the shores of complicated for a while now. Wait until I show you the verse in my purse."

"Who else have you spoken to?"

"Lady Duessa."

He sighs. "Only the dead can keep secrets. I often forget that."

"Turn that frown upside down, buddy, because I got an address and talked to a little bronze lady. What have you managed to come up with?"

"Nothing. You should stay out of this, Tess."

I ignore him and pull out my phone. "No word from Selena. I guess we're on our own. Lucian and I are going to meet with the supplier tonight."

Modred's face darkens. "That would be stupid. Even with a necromancer in tow—"

"Hey, nobody's towing me anywhere," Lucian interjects.

"We'll be out of sight," I say.

"I'm coming with you."

"Dude, we're fine."

"I am not asking. I am coming."

"I don't know," Lucian says. "You've got a loud aura. It increases the chances of the supplier noticing us."

"They won't sense me. If I wished it, neither of you would sense me, no matter how close I was."

"Okay, okay, everyone's aura is the cock of the walk. Let's not argue about this. Modred, I need you to translate something for me."

"Do we really have time for this?"

"It could be significant."

"I would prefer to spend some time with the text, if possible. Translating on-site seems vulgar."

I hand him the crumpled edge of my cell-phone statement. He peers at the verse. Then he hands it back to me.

"I believe it is a *jarcha*. An eleventh-century poetic fragment from Iberia. It's written in a mixture of Arabic, Occitan, and Gallician-Portuguese."

"Can you read it?"

"No."

"Shit. Really?"

"It's older than me. *Non me tanqas* could mean 'don't touch me.' "

"*Bastate* sounds like 'stop it,' " Lucian says. "That's all I can make out. Why are we looking at this poem?"

"Because this is what a CORE computer spit out when I asked it a question about Lord Nightingale."

"It gave you a *jarcha*?" Modred frowns. "That makes no sense."

"Welcome to my world."

"He was still human then," Lucian says. "Still Theresa of Portugal. Whoever planted the poem must know of his former life."

"But is it a joke?" I ask. "Or a password of some kind? I could ask Duessa, but she never tells me anything straight, and she already thinks that I'm way out of my depth."

"Quartilla might be able to read it," Modred says. "She's older."

"I'm a little weirded out by her finger-bone cuff links."

"She's actually not that bad once you get to know her."

"First things first. We're meeting Albert at the restaurant."

"Albert?"

"The zombie waiter."

"Lovely," he mutters.

On our way to the restaurant, I arrange several marbles. Lord Nightingale. The Seneschal. My mother. These people should not be related. As a necromancer, Lord Nightingale is connected to Pharmakon, but only obliquely. I guess my mother must have known the Seneschal, but what could his connection be to the drug? That was Mr. Corvid's world, not his. The Seneschal was more of a friendly uncle who collected antique weapons.

I have managed to read a bit about Theresa of Portugal. She was the bastard daughter of King Alfonso. She fought with her sister, Urraca, for control of peninsular Spain, and was eventually defeated by her own son. She died in political exile. It's hard to believe that this woman, looking slyly at me from a manuscript, could have become the person that I met, whose throne room was hung with glowworms. Theresa, you touched my hand. *Non me tanqas.* That was what Lucian said. *Don't let him touch you.*

We pick up Albert. He's nervous when he sees Modred, although the vampire barely notices him. Albert hands me a paper bag.

"The cook made you baklava," he says.

"Wow. Thanks."

"Do not eat that," Lucian murmurs.

We head to the apartment. It's a tidy walk-up, basically a shuffled house, with six mailboxes. We hang back while

Albert goes to the door. He opens the fourth mailbox and withdraws a parcel. He leaves our note, then hurries away. I don't blame him. I feel like we've chosen a pretty good spot, though. Modred has turned down his aura. We wait.

Ten minutes pass. Just as I start to think that we should have brought Chex Mix, the door opens. A guy in a mask walks out. He reaches into the mailbox and examines the note. We left a phone number that, should he call it, will connect him to the WestJet customer service line. He looks in our direction. The mask covers his face, but I notice that he's wearing an earpiece. I can't tell if it's a headset or a hearing aid.

He doesn't move for a few seconds. He's listening. Where have I seen a mask like that before? Then I remember: A necromancer who attacked me in Stanley Park was wearing a mask of similar design. Some kind of acid-etched metal. But he doesn't feel like a necromancer. What is he?

"We have to get out of here," Lucian says.

His words draw my attention away from the doorstep. When I look again, the man is gone.

"Where did—"

I don't finish the sentence. Something flashes just at the edge of my vision. I feel cold air. Then blood hits my face. Modred's blood. His face is covered in cuts. He barely flinches as they heal.

"Show yourself! This is cheap magic."

The cold brushes me. Then I feel a knife on my throat. He's holding me from behind. His grip is light, but there's something about his touch that's making me feel cloudy. I want to disarm him, but my body isn't listening. I reach for materia, but come up dry. Something's cutting me off. It has to be the knife.

A charm like that has a bitsy locus. It requires skin contact, and he's holding it steady. I go limp, which is practically the only thing I can do. He pulls me up, and the knife skips a beat on my skin. In that moment, I yell at the dust. *Go in his mouth!* It rises from the street and goes down his throat.

He gags and drops the knife. I pick it up and realize that it's rusted. It looks like it belongs in a museum. Or maybe in a demon hoarder's collection. As I'm thinking about this, I feel him messing with the warp of my spell. Then he sends the dust flying back at me. I call off the cloud, but in the second that it takes to do that, he's gone. Only the knife is left behind.

"Well," I say. "That happened."

"Discount spells," Modred says. "I feel like I need a shower."

I look at Lucian. "Why did you say that we needed to leave?"

"I knew he was getting ready for something."

"Yeah. But you knew before us, which is weird. Unless he was a necromancer."

He doesn't say anything.
"Did you know him?" Modred asks.
Lucian looks at me. He hesitates. Then he says:
"You just met my brother."

12

I call an emergency meeting at the house. This involves beer, potato salad, and two rotisserie chickens, since Mia and Patrick both happen to be home and we might as well do away with dinner. Modred abstains, which is probably better for all of us. I wait until everyone's finished before I turn to Lucian.

"So. Your brother's a dealer. How did that happen?"

"He's not a dealer. I mean, yes, sometimes he sells, but he's only ever dealt in party drugs before. Nothing like Pharmakon."

"Okay." Mia stands up. "This sounds like one of those discussions you'd rather I not be part of."

"You can go," Patrick says. "I feel like this is about to get awesome."

"You might as well stay," I tell her. "I can't protect you from hearing weird shit forever, and that's what our lives are about. Today, we discovered that Lucian's brother, Lorenzo, is both alive and pushing terrible drugs."

"He's not alive, strictly speaking—"

I raise one hand. "No. Enough with being cute. We're family. We can't have any more secrets."

"Just to be clear," Modred says, "I'm not family, and I don't really care about anyone here except for the Magnate. I'd actually like to go home. My face still hurts a little."

"You can't go," Patrick says. "I might have questions."

Modred exhales. "Of course."

I turn back to Lucian. "No more sidebars. If Lorenzo's harmless, why did he put a knife to my throat? A knife that I had to wrap in plastic and carry home in my purse, since the lab is going to want it."

"I don't know where he got that."

"But you knew he was dangerous. You said we had to leave."

"Yes. I know. I was paranoid. Lorenzo sort of collects spells. He has so many of them that sometimes he's like a walking curiosity shop, and not the kind with the cute mechanical pineapples. Like the spell on the knife that made you nearly pass out."

"I did not nearly pass out."

"You dropped like a sack of potatoes."

"That was a maneuver."

"Uh-huh. The point is that his spells are unpredictable. They're on permanent shuffle."

"You know, earlier, you said that you barely saw him. Now you seem to know a lot about his spell schedule."

"He has been texting me a little."

"I fucking knew it."

"Yeah. You knew it because you read one of them. You may have tried to mark it as unread, but all you did was flag the message."

"Crap. It was dark."

"Tess."

"I saw it by accident."

"You accidentally hit three buttons to read it?"

"I did it by instinct," I say lamely. "And besides, your privacy is no longer the point. Lorenzo is a criminal, and he was bold enough to attack Modred."

"It was more of a slap," Modred clarifies.

"How many spells did he have?"

"I counted three that were active," Lucian says. "Celerity, perplexity, and mass. He also had a passive counterspell that turned your dust back on you."

Mia gives me a look. "You threw dust at him?"

"I threw it in his mouth."

"Really, though? The rocks listen to you, and that's all you could think of? Why not spray him with a water bottle?"

"That's enough from the peanut gallery," I say. "Go to your room. I need you to translate something." I hand her the poem. "It's from the eleventh century. So far, all we've got is 'pretty' and 'don't touch.'"

"Tess," Modred says, "I'm by far the oldest thing in this room, and I speak a dozen languages. What exactly is she going to do?"

"She's going to use the Internet."

Mia takes the poem. "Cool. I'll let you know. Also, this seems like a good time to hit you up for money, since you probably wouldn't be asking me to do this unless it was something important."

I give her a twenty. "Please don't spend this on books. Buy something nice for yourself."

"Like hardcovers?"

She takes the money and vanishes upstairs. Parenting. It's all about improvisation and deli counters.

"Can I—" Patrick begins.

"No. Being part of this conversation is its own reward. Lucian's about to tell me what's going on with his brother."

"Can we agree to stop using the hostile third-person with my name?"

"Fine. Lorenzo's been texting you, and you haven't said anything. Nor have you ever, to this date, said anything about him actually existing. Which I think is more than a little shifty."

"He only started talking to me a few weeks ago. Honestly, I could just never think of a way to explain that he's kind of a ghost who lives in Trinovantum. You've been there once, and it didn't seem like the best time to ask you if you wanted to visit my brother who hates me."

"He can't possibly still hate you."

"He'll be a teenager forever. He can only leave once in a blue moon, wearing spells like a snowsuit."

"He seems comfortable enough visiting this city to have already made a tidy profit. I think the time to defend him has passed. We need to find him in Trinovantum before his shit drugs kill someone else."

"If you're going to Trinovantum, I want to come," Patrick says. "I think it would be super-educational."

"A thousand times no."

"Why do you have to crush my desire to learn?"

"Because it's not the safest place to be right now. Trust me. If you want to learn about something, figure out how I'm supposed to submit our taxes this year. I can't find a box for 'vampire dependent.'"

Mia comes downstairs. "That was diverting," she says. "Arabic, Gallico-Portuguese, and Old Castillian. I had so many windows open—it was awesome. Turns out, the poem was written by Yehuda Halevi. Here's the translation."

I read what she's written down:

Touch me not, my friend
Beneath such largesse
My little body is fragile
Enough, beautiful.

"Is it a love poem?" Modred asks.

"It could be a riddle," I say. "Riddles were huge back then. Maybe it really means 'helmet,' or 'rising loaf,' or something."

"It sounds dirty," Patrick says. "Like, *Dude, you're cute, but get your hand off my goods.*"

"This is why you're failing your second-year English class," Mia tells him. "You think everything's a gay joke."

"I've read Chaucer. Everything is a gay joke."

"My little body is fragile," I say, rising. "Maybe it's a musical instrument. Or something made of glass. Something easily broken." I walk over to the hutch, and laugh softly when I see the Seneschal's brass teapot. "I guess we might as well get one use out of you before you move to the evidence locker."

"I cannot believe they're asking for that back," Mia says.

"Yeah. The CORE has reasons that reason cannot know."

I throw two Lady Grey teabags into the pot and boil some water. I feel like Lucian's already doing that thing where he thinks if he's quiet enough, I'll forget that he lied to me. When the water's done, I pour it into the teapot, which howls and spits fireworks at me.

"Holy shit—"

I back away from the counter. The teapot is hopping mad and spilling water all over the place. It spins, faster and faster, until it becomes an arc of liquid brass. Then it settles down into the form of a small brass man wearing a toga. His ears steam. He spits out tea leaves and gives me a dirty look.

"You could have killed me."

"Oh—you're a Lar," I say.

"Of course. I'm the Seneschal's Lar."

"Two seconds ago, you were a teakettle."

"Two seconds? Try two years. That's how long I've been confined to your kitchen."

"How did you go to the bathroom?" Mia asks.

He ignores this. "My master gave me instructions. And since he's gone now, when I fulfill them, I'll be free."

"What were his instructions?"

"Two things. First of all, he says you must forgive your mother."

That stings. "I'll think about it. What else?"

"You must light a candle for him."

"That seems like an oddly Buddhist response to murder. But if that's his last wish, then I respect it."

"Murder?" The Lar gives me a strange look. "You think my master was killed? No, child. He was a phoenix. He burned, because his life had come to an end. That was his choice."

"But his cave looked like it was torn apart."

"I'm sure that when he died, creatures from all over the park came to rifle through his precious things, to sell them or destroy them. I suppose I'm the only thing left that he considered valuable."

"Well . . ." Mia says, a tad uncertainly. "If you want, you can still hang out in the hutch."

"I don't really have anywhere else to go."

"We're a bit like the Hotel California that way," I say.

I get up and rummage through one of the kitchen drawers until I find a candle. I light it and let it burn in the sink. It's a stray birthday candle, so it doesn't stay lit for long, but we all watch it. When it goes out, I reach for the electric kettle, hoping that our eulogy was good enough.

The animals are gathered in the conclusus when we arrive. The owls and nighthawks look down at the cats, while the frogs gossip. "Did you see her new pad? She's living in a bad part of the garden." The swans whisper, neck in neck, but I can't make out exactly what they're saying.

"What's going on?" I ask Lucian.

"Parliament. It looks like an emergency session."

"Haec vulnera pro libertate publica excepi," the horned owl begins. The nighthawks try to drown him out with hisses. "I shall speak. This is a time of great uncertainty. We need to take action."

A cat approaches the foot of the owl's tree. "What sort of action?"

"We must protect ourselves from hunters. And with all due respect, your people do not live here all the time, so you should not have a full vote."

"We do as much work as your people do in half the time."

"You do only what suits you."

"Let the cat speak," says one of the swans.

"Thank you," the cat says. "At any rate, the owl is right. Food is going to be scarce, and we are vulnerable, even here."

"Excuse me, your honors." Lucian steps into the circle of animals. "I don't mean to interrupt."

"Well, you are interrupting," the owl says.

"Yes. I apologize. But can you tell us what's happened?"

"The city is emptying out. Your people have moved on."

"Where's Lord Nightingale?"

"Fled. She was one of the first to go. She could not hold on to what was left of Trinovantum. The throne would not have her."

Lucian's eyes widen. "You're saying—everyone's gone?"

"Not everyone. A few have stayed behind. A brutal bunch, mostly, who hunt us and each other. And, of course, the ghosts haven't left."

"He brought a human with him," the owl says, noticing me for the first time. "This garden used to have standards."

"Hey." I step forward. "I'm barely human. Don't hold that against me. And, if it makes a difference, I know a leopard who's a lawyer."

"Her presence makes no difference," the cat says. "Let's prioritize. I will lead a scouting mission to the city in order to assess the palace larders."

"So, you're going to have a snack, followed by a nap." The owl shakes her tail feathers. "I get it. We all know how cats work."

"If nobody wishes to accompany, then I shall lead myself."

"We're going that way," Lucian says. "You're welcome to join us."

"Very well. I shall lead you there."

The cat turns and heads in the direction of the city. We follow. At first I wonder what he's going to do when we get to the water, but it's now so shallow that we don't have to summon a flower; there are rocks and exposed veins of black sand that we can walk on. The trees have lost their jewelry. Bright nets of glass are everywhere, like a shipwreck of Christmas ornaments.

"Where do the souls go when the glass breaks?" I ask.

"I don't know," Lucian says. "Hopefully somewhere nicer than this. It doesn't look anything like it did a few days ago."

"That's politics for you," says the cat.

We make it to the city gates, which yawn, unguarded. The night market has vanished. The square is empty. I hear something in the distance, but I can't identify it. We walk for a long time without encountering a single person.

Bleeding Out

I see a few shadows in doorways, but they're too quick for me to make them out. Maybe one of them is Lorenzo.

We reach the well of nightmares. Lucian grabs a container of apple slices from his knapsack.

"Wait," I say. "How's this going to work?"

"You will have to carry me." The cat looks me up and down. "I will endure it. Hopefully it won't last long."

We ride the nightmares. When we emerge at the entrance to the palace, I'm bleeding from multiple cuts. The cat drops to the ground, shakes himself, and begins composure-grooming.

"Are you okay?" Lucian asks.

"Let's just not talk about it ever."

We make our way through the empty palace. The armored spiders and the glowworms have all left. The stones aren't talking. I stare at the empty throne, which would have nobody else. I wonder what happened to his armor. Someone probably took it, along with the cushions.

"I shall examine the larder," the cat says. Before either of us can say anything, he's gone.

I follow Lucian to Lord Nightingale's chamber. It's been pretty well looted. There are a few books left, a bare mattress, and a frayed tapestry still hanging on the wall. I look closer. It's covered in dust, and the figures are indistinct. A line of text has been stitched into the corner.

"Can you read this?"

Lucian peers at the tapestry. "*Os alacrães son / ca*

dentro no coraçón / senti deles a espinha. That I recognize. It's from a *cantiga* by Alfonso X that Theresa loved. The speaker fears change. He feels like there's a nest of scorpions in his heart."

I look at the tapestry again. I see a nightingale suiciding in the border. Her song is a cloud of golden thread. I look at the ravened edges of the tapestry. I'm afraid to touch it, although the desire is powerful.

"My little body is fragile," I say.

I touch the nightingale's thorn. I feel its sting. A drop of my blood falls on the tapestry, and the threads come alive. The images change. I see five figures in a forest. There's an Iblis, a tall shadow, a winged lion, someone with claws, and a queen. Vampires gather around the edges of the clearing, while humans hide in the trees. As I watch, a new panel emerges. The queen has a different crown. The shadow is gone. A tower builds itself before my eyes, puffing out its balconies and turrets, until it divides into two, then three, then becomes a fortress. A city rises up around it. Necromancers made of thread roll out the streets. At its edges, the conclusus appears in knots of green and gold. The animals take their positions. The flowers are moored and ready.

"It's the creation of Trinovantum," Lucian breathes. "Lord Nightingale made a pact with demons. That must be where this all came from."

"There's the Manticore," I say. "And the Iblis who tried to kill me. And the one with claws. That's Mr. Corvid. And the shadow. It's—"

Before I can look closer, I hear a noise. Something flutters by me, and I go for my athame, but Lucian's faster. I see his hand move, and hear the sound of it connecting with something. I hear a curse. Then Lorenzo is on the floor, rubbing his eye. The mask is gone, and now I can see the resemblance. I imagine this is what Lucian looked like when he was seventeen.

"Stop this," Lucian tells him firmly. "It's not doing you any good. What are you doing sneaking around the palace?"

"I live here now." He stands up. "Nobody else does, so it's the ideal place. What are you doing here?"

"Looking for answers."

"The city's empty."

"We've been interviewing this tapestry," I say.

He looks at me. "Sorry about that thing with the knife. You startled me. I guess I panicked a bit."

"You're in a world of shit," I tell him. "We know you've been dealing Pharmakon. It was insultingly easy to find you, so I believe Lucian when he says that you're no expert in the drug trade."

"It was supposed to be fake! I mean, it looked fake. That stuff's always just been an urban legend that necromancers use to frighten their kids. *If you don't go to sleep, the day man will make Pharmakon out of you.* I didn't think it was actually real."

"Where did you get it from?" Lucian asks.

"A guy. I don't know his name. I ran into him in the

square, just as things were starting to get crazy, and he offered me a huge cut. I'm a ghost who can barely corporealize. I don't get offered a lot of good jobs."

"You're not the only ghost here," Lucian says. "You've got plenty of company. They don't feel the need to sell drugs."

"They don't do anything but moan and walk in circles. That's nice if you're into it, but I actually like consciousness. Not that you'd care."

"Lorenzo, I love you. I can't keep apologizing, okay? Right now, we need your help. Is there anything at all you can tell us about the person who gave you the Pharmakon? Was it a necromancer?"

"No. Demon." He peers at me. "Kind of smelled like you, in fact. Only he was a lot taller. Eyes like dirty ice."

"You've got to be kidding me," I murmur.

"What is it?" Lucian asks.

"The long shadow in the tapestry. The tall man. They're the same. Lorenzo's talking about my father."

"That hardly seems possible."

"Lucian, the Ferid are well traveled. We used to think they'd never been here, but I found an interview with a demon claiming to be one of them." I think about the figures in the tapestry again. "The Manticore, who said I was something. Mr. Corvid, who convinced me to remember. Lord Nightingale, who touched me when we first met. They'd all met before."

"You sound paranoid."

"No. No, I finally get it. This is why I was never supposed to meet him. This is what she was protecting me from. My father—"

I look at the tapestry again. A new city rises from the stitches of Trinovantum. A city by the sea. As I watch, the thread forms a tall building, a tower of a sort, but much more familiar. It's where I work. It's my life.

"Could he have made them both?"

Lucian looks at me. "What do you mean?"

Before I can answer, I hear something strange, like rats in the walls. My senses prick up.

"What is—"

"Get down!" Lucian screams.

The far wall of the chamber explodes. Moonlight streams in, and with it, something that looks like a funnel of blood and flame. My sister. I recognize her eyes, and the glow of her strange heart mechanism. She doesn't say anything. She simply heads straight for us. Her edges atomize whatever they touch. We run. She's fast, but chewing through the palace slows her down a bit.

"What is that?" Lorenzo screams.

"She's a Ferid," I say. "Worse. She's family."

We run and try to avoid the debris. Arcadia saws through a bone table and keeps going, like it was a tapa. We run down a tight corridor, and she follows, bringing down the walls with her.

"Lorenzo! Do you have any spells? Something to stall her, maybe, or calm her down?"

"No. All my spells are self-centered."

"Awesome."

"If we can reach the nightmares," Lucian yells, "we should be able to outrun her."

"Should be?"

"Just keep going!"

We run across the square, while Arcadia devours the paving stones behind us. She's like a flying mouth. A necromancer emerges from an alley that I thought was empty. He stares at Arcadia in shock. Then she goes right through him, leaving nothing behind.

We run through the gates, which are gone a moment later. All I can hear is the sound of her jaws. The nightmares are still tethered and waiting. The cat emerges from somewhere, licking her paws. Before she can protest, I scoop her up and jump on the nearest horse. I hold on to the nightmare's mane, choked with shells, while the cat digs his claws into my face.

We ride. The journey, as usual, makes me sick. When we get to the conclusus, Lucian yells to the animals: "Run! Everybody, run!"

I hear her cutting through trees. I hear the rage of the owls. Then we break out of the garden. We fall through space and onto the floor of Lucian's office, beneath the painting that granted us ingress.

"I don't think she can follow," Lucian says, breathing hard. "At least not through the painting. We never taught anyone else that trick."

I can see right through Lorenzo, to where the cat now sits, furiously cleaning his paws. Aside from being translucent, Lorenzo looks exactly the same. He examines the office.

"So this is your place. I figured it would suck."

"How long can you stay outside of Trinovantum?" I ask.

"A few hours. By that time, the cyclone should be gone."

"She's coming here," I say. "She's coming for me."

Lucian touches my shoulder. "You don't know that."

"What part about her trying to eat us did you not understand? The tapestry said it all. Those four creatures— Mr. Corvid, Lord Nightingale, the Manticore, and my father—they created both Trinovantum and the CORE."

"The CORE is a global corporation."

"So were the Knights Templar. Lucian, don't you get it? This is because of a medieval pact gone bad. They united to manage both demons and humans. Then we killed the Manticore. Arcadia killed Mr. Corvid. Now Lord Nightingale is dead. Both cities, Vancouver and Trinovantum, are under threat."

"Do you think he killed Theresa?"

"I don't know yet. What else could?"

"Not much. I don't understand. If he helped found Trinovantum, why would he want to see it abandoned?"

"Maybe he's done with it."

"And the Pharmakon?"

"I haven't figured out that part yet."

"You don't seem that great at solving mysteries," Lorenzo says.

I ignore him. "There are three wild cards in this. I'm the first. My mother is the second. Then Ru. We can't find her, but I do know where Ru is."

"So does Arcadia."

"That's why we're taking a cab. Come on."

13

Lucian and Lorenzo will not shut up in the back-
seat. I'm sitting between them, and we slide back and
forth as the cab exceeds escape velocity going down
Granville. Lorenzo doesn't want to let anything go. I'm
trying to think about two things at once. The first is the
possibility that I might be wrong. Maybe Arcadia has no
intention of coming for Ru. Maybe that wasn't even her
that we saw in Trinovantum. Can I really distinguish
between Ferid? I've only ever seen one. Still, I feel like
I recognized the twist of her heart, the particular weft of
her visible RNA. I stare at my phone. This is the second
thing. I can think of at least five people who I should be
calling right now, but my fingers aren't moving, only
Lucian and Lorenzo, who are fighting through me.

I'm struck by their resemblance. They argue in the way that's native to family members. Lorenzo frequently touches his hand to his nose with two fingers raised, then brings them down dismissively, which means "stupid." I can only understand about a third of what their hands are saying. It's begun to rain, and the traffic is getting ugly. Why haven't I called Selena? Maybe it's because I can't think of what to say. I'm not sure how to report what I saw in a tapestry. Is there even a form for that?

When Vancouver appeared in shades of thread I never knew existed, when Trinovantum rose around Theresa and her demons, that was the moment when things started to make sense. I had never really considered the nature of what I worked for, just as I did not often consider the lives of tapestries. The CORE was something I lived in, something I'd come to depend on elementally, like a shower curtain, a keyboard, a house whose bones you don't go looking for. But if what I'd seen was true, then this place that I worked for was actually a family business. My father had begun it centuries ago, with the help of a Manticore, a Bercilak-demon, and a necromancer. But why? I need a book on textile semiotics.

"Lucian," I say. "Why Theresa?"

"Excuse me?"

"Why would a self-named monarch make a demon's deal? I get what was in it for her, if she was able to unite the necromancers. What I don't understand is how she would have met those demons."

"We've never known anything about Lord Nightingale's past. Some thought that he wasn't really as old as he claimed to be. Under the light of Trinovantum, I suppose he was always indistinct. He could have been anyone. All we knew was that he'd always been there."

"He must have told you something about his past while the two of you were making bad decisions in Lisbon."

"We didn't talk very much. I could tell that he was tracking something, but he never told me what it might be. The city held a lot of memories for him. I guess that was when I first considered that he might really have been another person once."

"Not just another person. Another body. He went *Orlando* in the eleventh century, and nobody has any idea how. Did it never come up?"

"Frogs change their gender all the time," Lorenzo observes. "I don't see what the big deal is."

We get out a few blocks from the building and walk. All I can see are umbrellas and headlights. None of these people have any idea that we just came from an undead garden. They're thinking about bridge traffic. I'm thinking about my family. How will we stay together? Video conferencing will keep us alive, but it won't be the same. I won't be close enough to keep them safe. Arcadia is also my sister. My family staggers beneath entropy. No part of me is prepared for this reunion, but now we're in front of the building.

"Feel that?" Lucian asks.

I nod. "Vampires. Close, but out of sight. Could it be Modred and a friendly posse?"

"I don't think so."

"Yeah. Me neither."

"It might be worth it to call him, though. Or Patrick."

"Do that. I have to call—"

My phone goes dead. I hear people shouting, and realize that all of the lights are gone. The cars have stopped moving. There's no more neon. I see a crowd of people standing behind an automatic door that refuses to open, and others trapped halfway up escalators.

"It smells like electromagnetic interference," Lucian says.

"The lab has a fail-safe. It should have activated by now."

The windows of the CORE building stay dark. We get into the lobby, and people are everywhere, bumping into one another and trying to get their phones to work. The security desk is empty, and all the metal detectors have gone to sleep. We head for the emergency exit. We have to walk up fifteen flights of stairs. There are people coming down as well, but it's dark, and everyone is concentrating on their feet. We don't say anything to one another. It worries me that the emergency materia generator hasn't been activated. It worries me that I haven't heard from Derrick all day. It worries me that we never saw any of the vampires, even though we could feel them.

We reach the Forensic unit. The halls are full of people talking by the light of their athames. Selena sees me and walks over. I don't think she sees Lorenzo. It's dim, and he's pretty transparent.

She turns to me. "Where the hell have you been? You left without giving any kind of statement. We still can't track down your mother."

"Don't bother. You're not going to find her. Anyway, the Seneschal's death was a suicide."

"How do you know that?"

"I talked to his Lar. The bird was a phoenix."

"Wow. He more closely resembled a vulture."

"Maybe he'd let himself go. The point is that we came at this wrong. We thought his death was linked to the murder of Lord Nightingale, but it was random. He died of old age. Monsters trashed his place after, which is why it looked like a crime scene."

"I suppose a statue told you that as well?"

"No. Lucian's brother did, but that's a discussion for another day. What's wrong with the fail-safe?"

"It failed. Or rather, its connection failed. I've sent people to the subbasement to activate it manually, but it's hard to communicate with them. Our telepaths are working overtime."

"Is Derrick here?"

"I'm not sure. I haven't seen him. At the moment, I'm more interested in why you and Lucian are here."

"Well, that story begins with a tapestry, and ends with the possibility of my sister killing us all. I'm not sure how to put it into a nutshell."

"Why don't you try?"

"Fine. All I really understand is that the Ferid are behind this. They murdered Lord Nightingale. I don't know how, but they're pretty much the only ones who could have."

"This seems elaborate, even for you."

"I don't know any other way to explain it."

"We've heard nothing from them. As far as we know, they never tried to get Ru back. Why would they do this?"

"I—" All I can do is blink. "I don't really know why. I just know. They're written all over this, somehow."

"Plus," Lucian adds, "one of them chased us through Trinovantum."

Selena stares at me. "You didn't think to lead with that?"

"I was getting there!"

"There was a thing with a textile," Lucian says. "You really had to be there. But some of what she's saying actually makes sense."

"Thank you. Right now, we have two problems. The first is that there are vampires clustered outside. Something's up, and there's no way of contacting the Magnate. I think we have to assume that they're hungry and hostile."

"We have people keeping an eye on them," Selena says. "Probably not enough people, though. What's the other problem, aside from the fact that this power outage is destroying whole rooms full of trace evidence?"

"It's what I think might be causing the blackout."

"Please don't say it's the Ferid."

"Okay. I won't. But it is. I think they're coming for Ru. And for me. And possibly for my mother."

"You're teetering on incoherent."

"Well, that feeling is kind of my life. Where's Ru?"

"In his suite, as far as I know. I haven't seen him. Tess, why would they come for him now?"

"All I understand," I say, "is that, when Lord Nightingale died, a pact died with him. I think the Ferid are cleaning house. Trinovantum has lost all of its necromancers. Mr. Corvid no longer controls the drug trade. Even the Manticore doesn't scare us at bedtime anymore. All the other monsters have fled. The Ferid are the only ones left."

"As a species, they don't live anywhere near us."

"No. Not yet."

"And you're confident of this—because you saw a tapestry."

"Think of it this way, boss. If a cosmic shit-storm was going to descend on anyone in this building, who would the target be? I think we both know the answer to that. The lightning loves me."

She sighs. "All right. Get Ru, and I'll evacuate the building."

"And send all those people into the streets? That's probably what the vampires are hoping for."

"You could send them out slowly," Lucian says. "With escorts. It will take longer, but they'll be less vulnerable."

Selena turns to address the crowd. "Everyone get into threes. One athame per group, set to flare. Let's keep this nice and orderly. We're going to pick up everyone we see along the way and coordinate a safe exit."

We head to Ru's suite. The door is open, but he's not there.

"This is way better than my apartment," Lorenzo says.

"At least rent is low now."

"It's virtually nonexistent. But everyone still fights over property."

"All right." I stare down the hallway. "If I were a kid who could walk on walls, and the power was out, where would I go?"

"What exactly makes you think that the Ferid are coming for him?" Lucian asks. "So far, all you've got are vampires and a blackout. Selena was right. They haven't made a peep about him staying in the lab for months."

"He and his brother saw something. Basuram suggested that it was an experiment, something to do with long-distance travel. I think he's on a list of loose ends that they need to annihilate."

"Including you?"

"Well, it's family. You're never quite sure how they really feel about you. Maybe Arcadia was tearing through your old city on a whim, and we happened to run into each other. But she came through that wall like a bat out of hell. She saw me and didn't stop coming."

"You're sure," Lucian says, "absolutely sure, that the shadow you saw in that tapestry was your father, and not something else?"

"No. I can't swear it. But I'd like to think that I could recognize my father's shadow. I've seen it enough. He sold drugs to Lorenzo, which connects him with Trinovantum. He's pretty much always on the edge of things. And now my murderous funnel of a sister wants to get rid of the bastard daughter."

"You know," Lorenzo says, "this is starting to sound like less of a forensic thriller and more of a science-fantasy."

"I don't have time to worry about the genre of this crisis. Our lab isn't equipped to analyze the Ferid. Ru's DNA practically broke our machines. The problem is that we got used to dealing with local demons, and the Ferid are global. They're capitalists, and they obviously don't give two cyclonic revolutions about us."

"I'm bored," Lorenzo says.

Lucian's about to retort, but I cut him off. "Lorenzo, do you think you have any spells that could help us?"

He brightens. "A few, actually. I've got feather-fall, limited invisibility, super-fast hands—"

"Let me use limited invisibility. I can tell my athame to remember it. Air charms are probably my weakest area."

He draws out a thin chain of materia, which he drapes over my athame. The knife eats the spell. I'll have to wait about twenty minutes until it's properly digested, but it could come in handy later.

"We need to reach the fail-safe," I say. "I know it's in the subbasement, but that's all."

"I'll scout ahead," Lorenzo says. "It will be more inter-esting." Then he evaporates into the floor.

"I like him."

"He has his moments."

"I don't think he hates you anymore."

"That's only because you couldn't understand our con-versation."

"I'll just go ahead and be optimistic anyway."

It's slightly heartbreaking walking down so many stairs after we worked so hard to climb them. If they weren't such shitty concrete, they'd probably have the presence of mind to laugh at our misfortune. We get to the lobby, which is slowly emptying. Outside, I see a typical maneuver in action. There's a burst water main on one side of Granville and a sparking cable on the other, neither of which was there before. Agents are escorting people out of their vehicles and taking them to safety. I can still feel the vampires, but they've divided. Where did the other half go? It's a question I'd like answered sooner rather than later.

We go through the emergency exit and down two flights of stairs. The quality of the air changes. It's thin-ner, colder, and I can smell industrial cleaning products, which puts us on the morgue level. Another two flights of steps, and we're past the data archive and reference library. We come to a locked door. I'm about to touch it, stupidly, like someone who's forgotten about a hot ele-ment. Before I can, however, Lorenzo appears.

"Do not think about touching that," he says. "Listen. It's putting out as much energy as a respectable white hole."

I inch closer and examine the lock. It's made of old metal that's been painted to look new. I might be able to work with it.

"Okay," I say. "Let's come at this logically. First of all, door, I'd like to greet you as a wielder of materia. I'd also like to remind you that my family has close ties with the wind, the seas, and the elder rocks, which means that you can trust me. I get that you were told not to open. But this is an emergency. The building might be under attack, and we need to activate the fail-safe. Surely, you were never ordered to put your own substrate in jeopardy."

I protect.

"What do you protect?"

The deep basement.

"Right. I respect that. But there's something in the deep basement that we need to protect all the other basements, and the doors and carpet and everything else that makes the building possible. We just need to turn that thing on."

Others asked, but were dismissed.

"Dismissed how?"

Made to leave.

"But no killing, right?"

The door doesn't answer.

"Okay. I have a special deal for you, because you're

such a good door. If you let us in, I promise to remove that awful paint from your lock. I'll sand you down and give you oil."

I want a mural.

"Done. We'll paint something nice and everyone will stop to check you out, just like they used to before you were moved to the subbasement."

The door considers my offer. Then it opens.

"We're in your debt."

I want a mural.

"Right. Message received."

We go down a hallway. I can smell iron in the air, and something else, which I can only describe as a dryer sheet gone bad. Then I smell vampires. I hug the wall and take Lucian's hand before calling in the limited invisibility charm. My athame casts it, and we try not to move. Three vampires walk by. The Pharmakon has made them look slightly prehistoric, and extremely amped up. I think we could take them, but I remember how unpredictable the vampire was who attacked me on the beach. I don't want to risk it.

They pass us and continue south. We go north. I keep trying to hear something from the fail-safe, at the very least the song of weak radioactivity, but all I get is static. I stop for a moment to listen more closely. It's like standing in a blizzard. I close my eyes and cast a thought into the nullity:

Derrick.

There's no response at first. Then I hear something extremely faint. I hold on to an image of Derrick and cast my thought again. The faint noise comes back. I listen closely. He's saying something, but I can't make it out. I give up and listen for the fail-safe again, which yields only static.

"We could use Miles in this situation," Lucian observes. "He'd be able to chat with the generator."

"That's funny," Lorenzo says. "I almost met a guy named Miles the other day, but then I lost my nerve and left the café."

Lucian frowns at him. "Why were you at a café?"

"I was waiting for the ghoul, and I had some time to kill. I went to a café on Commercial Drive and noticed a deaf guy who was totally into his smartphone. I don't meet a lot of deaf people, and he looked young, so I almost made myself semi-visible, like, so I could talk to him. But then his boyfriend came back, and was like, *Miles, stop reading; pay attention to me.*"

"Was his name Derrick?"

"Yeah. Miles wasn't really paying attention, but when the boyfriend looked in my direction, I thought he could almost see me. So I left. I made sure to walk through both their coffees, though, which makes them gross."

"You practically touched them." I'm captivated by the idea of my family meeting Lucian's, if only through a weak electrical charge. The diss of a ghost. Then I remember, for the first time in days, what Derrick told me after he examined Lord Nightingale's body. That memory. "Lorenzo, what was Miles wearing?"

"I don't usually pay attention to what dudes are wearing."

"What color was his shirt?"

"I think it was blue."

"You don't think. You know." I stare at him. "You were at the library that night. When you passed by Miles, you picked up the smell of his shirt. It would have been nothing to most people, but Derrick recalled it instantly. You left that stolen smell behind without even knowing it."

Lucian's eyes widen. "Lorenzo, is this true?"

He's silent for a moment. Then he says: "He was dead when I got there. I was at the library looking for a cookbook. It's easy to manifest because the university is so high above sea level. When I realized who it was, I didn't know what to do, so I hid and watched. Your people came. I was surprised to see the boyfriend there. He almost saw me again, but I kept still."

"Lorenzo, if that's true, then you were the first person to arrive on the scene. Did you sense something? Did you see a possible weapon?"

"No. I felt sad, because he was kind to me. I felt the silence of his death. But there was nothing else."

"Great. First you show up at a crime scene; then you start selling drugs. This is the kind of story that conservative moms love to hear."

"Look. I barely dealt them, okay? The weird guy gave

them to me, and I gave them to the squid. I think a vampire bought most of it."

"Which vampire?"

"I never met him. But the ghoul said that he runs a community center."

I go cold. "Are you talking about Modred?"

"I don't know his name. The ghoul couldn't even understand what he was saying half the time."

"That's him." I turn to Lucian. "Modred bought the Pharmakon. He's the one who's dosing them."

"That doesn't seem like something that he would do."

"Neither of us really know him. Patrick looks up to him, but he's never been the best judge of character. He's too kind. When Modred and I were at the party, he made certain that I never spoke with Quartilla, who was probably the only other person there who knew anything. He kept telling me to leave it alone and let him sort it out. I was right about him managing me."

"Do you trust anyone?"

"Sure. I trust lots of people. But I live with those people. If they were lying to me, I'd realize it. Modred is hard to read on a good day, and when he reaches for the poker face, good luck. I think that he's been working against us from the start."

"Vampires are tools," Lorenzo says.

"Well, if that were the case, we'd have nothing to worry about. But the vampires who just walked by are blitzed on Pharmakon and looking for a fight. I already used up our limited invisibility, so next time they appear, we'll have to think of something while running."

We continue down the passage. Eventually, it narrows and ends in a small enclosure. There's a hole in the floor with a ladder leading down. I lay my fears about submarines aside, and use the ladder. It leads to a chamber that's mostly dark, save for a pair of green eyes, which fasten on me the instant my feet touch the ground. I light my athame.

"Ru! We've been looking all over for you."

"I've been here," he says. "This is the safest part of the building. The storm outside is getting worse."

I look around. In the center of the room is a glass chamber, which is empty. My athame starts to crackle as it picks up a bit of weak radiation still settling over the area.

"Is this the fail-safe?" I ask.

"It was," Ru says. "But someone has stolen the battery."

"Awesome." I turn to Lucian. "If we can't activate the building's defenses, we're humped. Anything can get in, if it hasn't already."

"It's me that they want," Ru says.

"Actually, they want both of us."

"Did you also see something that you were not supposed to?"

"No. I'm just lucky that way." I get down on one knee. "I may not be able to turn the power back on, but I can wake the building up. Everyone kneel and join hands."

"I'm not solid enough to kneel," Lorenzo says.

Ru notices him for the first time. "Where did he come from?"

"Everybody just fucking kneel. Now. And join hands."

Ru takes my hand. "How do you wake a building up?"

"Like this."

I touch my athame to the ground.

Wake up.

Floors, wake up. Windows, listen. Now is the moment to be who you are. Brackets, ducts, and pipes of every angle. Insulation. Carpet fibers, granite countertops, sleeping drywall: Now is the time to be. All you staples, frames, and hidden rebar, wake up. It's a beautiful night for a battle. Marble, reveal your striae. Iron, remember your birth. Floors, shed your laminate; remember your ancestors who were Viking ships. Glass, look up and receive the moon. Walls, guard us and forgive us.

Oh, my building. You have known me since I was young, and before that, you knew my mother. I love you. Wake up and show yourself. Let your surfaces roar. Let the basements bare their teeth. Let every trace within you, every piece of evidence, wake up and remember what it is. Oh, my building. Now is the moment. You are not simply one building in a terminal city. You are my building, and I see your naked battlements. We matter to each other. We are tame to each other, like princes and foxes. I would recognize you in any light. Oh building, we're so close—look, we're touching now. Wake up, beautiful.

It works. The building rouses. A current passes through it, and suddenly, I can see the earth materia in the walls, clear as gold in water. I hear the thundering of the windows as they come undone. I feel everything around me remembering its potential.

Then I hear a sound that does not belong.

It's like a roaming jigsaw.

Arcadia is outside.

She appears in the entrance, flushed and hungry. Detritus whirls around her. The building isn't just allowing itself to be devoured. It's throwing things at her. It's screaming at her. But it's not enough.

She is death in a doorway. She is more powerful than whatever miracle battery we were hoping for. She wears her helices on the outside of her body, which glow, like a necklace of coals. Her aperture seems big enough to swallow the entire room. I raise my athame. I don't feel confident.

"Oh," she says. "Good. Both of you are here."

"You will not take me," Ru says. "I will not return to my world in chains, as your experiment."

"You misunderstand." Arcadia ignores the outraged chairs and filing cabinets that swirl around her. "I have not come to collect you. Why do you think I am here, Tess?"

"Because you can't let anything go?"

"Because the peace is over. The agreement that we made with your ancestors has become void. Just like Lord Nightingale, the Bercilak-demon, the Manticore—all dust. We tried it your way for a thousand years. We let you handle things. You could barely protect yourself from the night. And the necromancers were no better. They wilted after centuries of being ruled by a despot."

"And your plan now is—what—to kill us both? You're really going to kill your own sister?"

"You were never part of the family."

"No. The problem is that you could never keep me out. I kept looking for my father, even after your nightmares, even after my mom lied to me to make things better. I kept looking. That only proves that I really am his daughter."

"You were never anything."

"That Manticore told me that I was. Mr. Corvid told me that I was. Even Basuram recognized me. Obviously, I'm something, Arcadia. That's what pisses you off. I matter. All of my families love me, or else I would never have survived this long. Even he loves me."

"He sent me to kill you."

"I don't think so. He would have come himself."

"I am his general. I make these decisions."

"Tess—" Lucian begins. There's fear in his voice.

"No." I raise my athame higher. I feel the building listening, ready to follow my move. I'm not afraid. "I said this was the moment, and it is."

"When I pass through you," Arcadia says, "it will be like you never existed. No part of you will remain as evidence. Are you ready?"

I feel both Ru and Lucian drawing power on either side

of me. I feel the presence of those who love me, even if I can't hear them. I remember what I thought when I first stepped into this building, years ago, when I was so young and nothing but beautiful doors. I'm thinking the same thing now.

This really is what I was born to do.

"Are you ready?" I ask her.

Uncertainty flashes across her eyes for a second. Then she moves. I feel the heat of her edges. Oh, my sister. You can take me, but not them. You will never have my little gods. I love them too much. I open myself completely to every substrate. I whisper to my athame:

Now is the moment. When I die, everything that I am will burst into light and angry neutrinos. It belongs to you. The building is listening. You must strike with all the power I have left. You must end her.

I look at Lucian. Everything I can't say is in my glow. I smile. I beg the building to protect them both.

Arcadia falls upon me, and I aim for her heart.

Light breaks everywhere. I feel incredible pain as my athame sings. My bones are wind. I let myself scatter.

But I don't. I spin. I am also a cyclone, or part of me is. Every molecular bond shears from the impact. I spin until our orbits match, until I can see the division of her rings. I flatten to a wave. I'm about to lose myself completely in her, when a voice says:

"Stop."

14

I stop spinning, but I don't know if I'm alive or dead.

The pins and needles are so bad that I can hardly move. I feel cuts on my face, my arms, every part of me, but they're shallow. I'm looking into Arcadia's eyes. The brilliance of her hate drives her, and she continues to circle, but she's slowed down. I look to my left, which takes a lot of effort. Lucian and Ru are unconscious on the ground. Most of the debris that was whirling around my sister has now settled to the floor. There are enough mundane objects to build several offices, but they're burnt and pulverized, so you'd have to get creative if you were going to try.

"Thank you for listening," the building says.

The lights are still out, but there's a voice coming through the PA system. The voice speaks slowly and precisely, as a person often does when using a second language.

"That was ugly for a moment. It was difficult to tear you apart. But I see that the damage is minimal."

"Who is speaking?" I ask. "Is this the building?"

"You know who I am."

My breath catches. "Father?"

"You look good. I see you have grown up."

"Are you here?"

"Yes and no. I am here enough for us to talk."

"Then please tell her to stop trying to kill me."

"Arcadia, you should go."

"Father—"

"You have done enough. Go."

She begins to say something. Then she just looks at me, once, before spinning herself out of sight. All the metal objects breathe a sigh. Lucian and Ru show no signs of waking up. It's just me and his voice.

"Is the tapestry right?" I ask.

"It certainly tells a good story. Did you like it?"

"I suppose you planted the poem."

"No. That was her idea. Obviously, there could be no public information about who she really was. But she did like poetry, and she wanted to leave a riddle. I think it is safe to say that most people would not translate a fragment written in eleventh-century Zaragoza. But you did."

"Mia did."

"I would like to meet her someday."

"I don't think I want her anywhere near you."

"I hold no malice toward your family. On the contrary. I am proud of what you have created. I am glad that you are not alone. You cannot imagine how lonely it is to be this old."

"We're not talking about your golden years. Did you kill Lord Nightingale?"

"Yes."

"Why?"

"Because he asked me to."

"He asked you to cut his throat?"

"You have to understand that when I met Theresa, she was out of her mind. She was destroyed by her own family. Her brother, Alfonso, had routed her in battle. She had lost Portugal, and all she had to look forward to were days of exile with her consort, far from the politics of Lisbon. That was why she turned to necromancy. She wanted the throne back at any cost."

I frown. "But—she died, became a man, and moved to Trinovantum. What did that have to do with getting back Portugal?"

"Nothing. When we gave her the city to rule, she forgot about her old throne. Her body did not change immediately. But over the centuries, she lost her old self and took on a new one. The city and its power transformed her into a king. But a king should not rule for a thousand years. They lose their stomach and make bad decisions."

"They make treaties with vampires."

"Exactly."

"So this is a conservative thing. Lord Nightingale wanted to bring demons and humans closer together, but it was more profitable for you to keep them apart. I suppose you killed Luis Ordeño for his part in that as well."

"You are as paranoid as your sister. No. Ordeño died because he was trying to make a deal with the Manticore. Like many others, he thought he could use the old creature's power, and that was his mistake. I have never been opposed to integration. Theresa was the one who resisted the treaty, as she resisted change of any kind."

"But I'm supposed to believe that she asked you to kill her."

"She called for me. I found her in the library, reading a book of *jarchas*. She said she was too tired. It wasn't fair that the others had finally died and she was still here. She knew that her people were changing, that her city no longer obeyed her. When I looked into Lord Nightingale's eyes, I saw the old, mad Theresa staring back at me. I knew what she was asking."

"You cut her throat and turned her into Pharmakon? She was a thousand. She deserved better."

"I didn't cut her throat. I kissed her. That's what always happens when we touch someone filled with carbon. I could have kissed her with my mask on, but she wanted honesty. She wanted rest."

"You stole her leukocytes."

"Tessa, there is no such thing as Pharmakon. What I gave to the ghost was a mixture of phencyclidine and embalming fluid. It makes vampires hallucinate and maximizes their anger response. They are not magical or invulnerable. They are hungry and confused."

"Modred wouldn't do that to his people."

"Modred wants to be Magnate. He used to be a knight. Obviously he is tired of taking orders from an undergraduate."

"So—" I feel like my brain is going to explode. "This isn't a takeover. You're just going to stand by and let the vampires tear each other apart."

"Ideally, they were supposed to go after the necromancers, but they fled at the first sign of trouble. Now they will have to work things out among themselves, which usually requires a slicker if you happen to be watching."

"I don't get it. Why would you create all of this, let it run for a thousand years, and then just watch it burn?"

"You do not get it, as you say, because you are in it. We are outside. We have a bigger picture to consider. By the eleventh century, vampires and death-dealers were annihilating the human population. The animals and the old demons knew that something needed to be done. So an agreement was made. Those who practiced necromancy were given Trinovantum. This allowed humans with other magical aptitudes to safely emerge, and they were encouraged to form a collective. They called it *core*, after 'heart,' but eventually, like all things, it became an acronym."

"CORE."

"Regulation enterprise." I detect a note of dark humor in his voice. "Our first lesson to them was that magic could not be controlled, only seduced. But humans like to form committees, and committees like to regulate. Before contact, the first peoples that we dealt with in this country were respectful of this knowledge. The foreigners from Europe were not. Their committees tended to involve bonfires. But free will is tricky that way, and magic is a louse that hates to discriminate. We had to give them all a chance."

"And now—what—you're going to dismantle an ancient culture of workers, artists, and scholars because they made bad decisions? You're going to judge us for our mistakes when all you did was sit on a faraway star and watch?"

"I was never that far away. But don't you think a thousand years is a generous stretch of time? The problem is that you spent the first six hundred of those years burning witches, and the remaining centuries pondering your own genes while magic waited for you to do something."

"You're telling me that none of the cores in the world have impressed you? Not even the one in Stockholm?"

"It has all been micromanagement. We changed the nature of evolution for you. Vampires were hunting you. Humans were misusing necromancy, disturbing the dead.

Magic was killing you, because you were weak and did not respect it. The cores were an experiment. They have all failed, but none so spectacularly as yours, I think."

"You're not seeing any of the good things. There are brave materia-wielders and agents, people who make magic look like poetry. I still believe in the oath that I took."

"Have you never enlisted materia for selfish means? Have you never harmed a normate, never revealed yourself? Have you always been a bulwark against the suffering of others?"

"I'm not perfect."

"Of course not. Prisms are perfect. You have to be flawed, but these flaws are not what disappoint us. The real issue is that people with magic have proven themselves to be just as selfish and destructive as people untouched by it. The cores of the world were designed not only as schools, but as courts. Your task has always been to investigate death by magic. But you seem to cause as many deaths as you solve."

"Our numbers are a lot better than that."

"If they were, we would not be having this conversation."

"Okay. You're pissing me off now." I try to look for some person who's talking, but the room is dark and I'm alone. Ru and Lucian are still out. All I can do is pretend that he's in front of me. "The last few days have been a case in point. The lab wasted a lot of energy on investigating the death of Lord Nightingale. You couldn't have just told us that it was a suicide?"

"We don't have time to report the obvious to you."

"The whole time, I suppose we were never really investigating anything. We were the ones under investigation. A queen and an old bird died, and in reality, it had nothing at all to do with us."

"That is what solipsism gets you."

I raise my athame. It illuminates the room, but I'm still talking to nothing. At least I could see Arcadia.

"Why are you here?" I ask again.

"To gather data. Things are obviously winding down here, and a report will need to be made. This isn't the only world where materia exists. You've seen glimpses of a few, but believe me when I say that they are uncountable. Magic is everywhere, Tessa. People need to learn how to treat it."

"Does that mean you've got bastard daughters across the cosmos?"

This silences my father's voice for a second. Then the building says:

"No. You are my only child. You were a mistake, but I'm glad that I made you."

"How does something like you make a mistake like me?"

"Your mother and I struck by accident. Neither of us expected it. When she realized, after, what I was, she tried to find me, but your sister got to her first. Diane was lucky to get away from her that night."

I realize that what he's saying is true. She could have sustained those injuries while running from Arcadia. She knew that part of my sister lay inside me, that the column of fire chasing her through the streets would someday be in my blood. Still. She gambled on love.

"I think Arcadia hates you more than me," I say.

"That is sadly true."

"Is it because she feels betrayed?"

"No. I believe it is because she wanted a much better life than the one that I offered her. If anything, she envies you."

"She was going to eat me."

"In some cultures, that is a sign of great respect."

"Father." I close my eyes. I try to imagine what he looks like, beyond what I've seen in dreams. I imagine how he might spin. "When I ask you what you're doing here, what I mean is, what's going to happen?"

"That will depend on which vampire wins. It will also depend on whether the necromancers come back to roost in this city. Then it will be as if a thousand years had never passed."

"That's just *Thunderdome*."

"I suppose the people with magic will either rise to the occasion, or be hunted to extinction. Demons will move unchecked through the city. It should be interesting to watch."

I've spent my whole life waiting to stand up to my father. What surprises me now is how much I love him, unexpectedly, old and dangerous thing that he is. Part of what made me, and, in some way, beautiful. His logic is not alien to me at all. I understand the choices that he needs to make. Love has always embarrassed me. But I feel it for this voice without a body.

"You will not stand back and watch," I say. "You know that we deserve more chances. And I'm not even talking about the whole world. Have you seen this city, with its bridges and its glass and its roots in the ocean? I've spent my life protecting it."

"Perhaps you need a new life."

"No way. I'm still learning to drive this one."

"Give me a reason, then. Why shouldn't I let it all end?"

It's an honest question. We've clearly fucked around with our magic; there's no arguing that. If we'd been better investigators and more skilled managers, there wouldn't be coked-out vampires on Granville Street right now. Why shouldn't it end? That's precisely the choice that Selena's offering me, and maybe she's right. Maybe we all need to retire.

But even as I think this, I don't believe it. To me, magic has always felt like nothing more than our ability to listen. Tuning in to the stones and having a conversation with fire was possible, on a preconscious level, for everyone, but only people like me could actually convince the elements to do things. People like Lucian, now sweetly asleep next to a horned boy, can argue with death, but more often, they spend most of their time just listening to it. I'm not ready to give up that conversation.

"We can change," I say. "We can become better listeners."

My father considers this. "You would change your core?"

"I'll lead it."

"What leadership skills do you possess?"

"I'm the head of a family."

"You wish to depose your supervisor?"

"Not at all. I'll be the boss, but Selena will still be my boss. I'm sure that can go in a rider somewhere."

"You are serious."

"You're all up in my city's grille. You think we're messing around, but I know exactly how hard we work every day, just to connect. I'm not going to step aside and let you stop our pilot light. If change is what it takes, then I'll be it."

"Who will listen to you?"

"The real question is, who won't listen to Selena?"

"I suppose she is like family to you."

"I think she sees me more as an annoying stepchild. But I do know that she'll help me. She'll need more office space, though."

"What makes you think that you can change anything at all?"

"Let's just say that, however complicated my childhood was, I came out of it with confidence. If I can raise vampires, I can raise a new core. If it catches on, maybe it'll spread to Alberta. Who knows? The point is that I can do it."

My father is silent. Then he asks: "Do you think you have learned magic's lessons?"

"How many are there?"

"Six."

"Oh. Well, it's possible."

"I will give you a choice, then. You can say good-bye to the experiment and return to your family. The core will fall, but you and those you love will be safe. I can promise you that, at least."

"What's the other option?"

"Dance with me."

"You're not even here."

"I will undress. But you must also. You must be Ferid, and for that, you need to spin until you achieve grace. If you have learned magic's lessons, you should be able to do this and survive. If not, you will detonate and consume the building, in which case, nothing changes."

"That seems like a bit of an asshole move on your part. Couldn't my test involve levitating a feather?"

"Spin or fail," he says.

"Okay. I choose to spin."

The light of my athame goes out.

I hear a mighty wind. In the dark of the room, my father is a storm. I feel myself becoming clouds. It hurts, but I let myself unravel, as cloth must. As I start to spin, I think about magic's lessons.

Death, you taught me that our ghosts forgive us, that entropy sleeps next to us all, that everything will one day be trace.

Thought, you taught me that sleep is precious, that telepaths are people who put up with a lot, that memory dies if you don't palpate it.

Earth, you taught me about centers and rifts, that stones worry about us, that our passions leave a record.

Water, you taught me silence, that our beautiful mothers are always fishing for us, that love is damp.

Fire, who I was once so scared of, you taught me that all our carbon has been through more than we could possibly imagine, that so many warm things are hard to let go of, that a determined spark can get a lot done.

And air, which I give myself to now, you taught me that birds see everything and still pardon us, that we're all barely here, that I can be anything because I have been a storm.

I may not have learned magic's lessons by heart, but I can read the sheet music. I can get by. I can dance, because my father is leading.

I peel off my rind and turn faster in his hands. The air sings to me as I come apart. I see Lorenzo. He's screaming something at me, but I can't hear. I turn and I turn and then I explode.

Remainder

We're nearly done packing. I say "we," but Mia's the one who's actually leaving, and she's done the least amount of packing possible. She sees herself in more of a supervisory position. Patrick and Lucian get to do most of the heavy lifting, which includes her library (not going to fit in the car), DVD collection, and Hefty cinch sacks full of clothes. It's still warm outside. Kevin Johansen plays on the radio. *Si no tiene logo / falta poco / saravarava.* Don't worry if you don't have a label. Good vibes. *Saravarava* indeed.

"How many hardcovers do you own?" Patrick exhales as he lifts a nearby box, which has been madly taped. "Please, promise me that when you get to Toronto, you'll buy a Kindle."

"I'll do no such thing," she says. "I like the smell of books, and that's that. Plus, you have vampire strength, so use it."

"I'm about to use it to knock you through a wall, sassy."

My mother steps into the living room. "No fighting. This is Mia's last day with us."

"That's right." Mia kisses Patrick on the cheek, which almost makes him drop the box. "You're gonna *miss* me. Because you *loooove* me."

"Shut up, sprat."

My mother gives me a look. Something like, *Aren't they interesting?* It's a covert attempt to set off my biological clock, but I ignore it. Lucian and I aren't ready for a baby. We've already got a vampire, a house god (who loves polishing everything in the house), and a dog whose person spends most of his time here. Even with Mia gone, the house will never be silent. Which I suppose is how I like it. Not loud, per se. Just full.

I don't know what made her choose the University of Toronto over Berkeley, Brown, and all the other schools that she applied to. It's still far away, but at least she's still on my side of the border. Most likely, she used a calculation to determine who had the best courses in Everything Studies, and U of T won out, but I'd still like to think that a part of her wanted to remain close.

When I stopped spinning, everything was different. Lucian and Ru woke up, rubbing their eyes, like Miranda on her island suddenly realizing how vast the ocean was, how everything could be new. The lights returned. I finally realized what Lorenzo, barely corporeal, had been screaming: *Don't forget who you are.* I guess I didn't.

Hand in hand in shadow, we walked up to street level, and couldn't believe the scene. It was the Stanley Cup riots with vampires everywhere, tweaked out, turning on one another. Patrick and his crew were trying to corral them. Modred, I guess, had fled. Patrick told me later that they'd faced each other in single combat, but Modred hesitated. Perhaps he didn't have it in him to strike down his student. Now he would always be an apostate, banished from the vampire nation for treason.

Water arced in the air. A bus was turned over on its side, like an angry turtle, throwing off sparks. Selena was directing traffic, her athame blazing as she used it to draw arrows of light. When she saw me, one eyebrow raised in a question. *What happened to you?* It would take the next few weeks to properly answer her. But I did know that I'd won the argument with my father. The vampire coup would not inspire epic Anglo-Saxon poetry. When the sun set, Patrick was still in charge, and everyone knew it.

And my mother appeared, running across the dangerous street.

"Tess! Are you okay?"

I don't think I've ever loved her more than I did in that moment. I grabbed her and held on for dear life.

"Where have you been all this time?"

"I got sucked into watching *The Tudors* and ignored the phone. You have no idea how great this season is." She surveys the street. "I've obviously missed something, though."

"You're damn right you did! I talked to Dad."

"Well." She smiled. "I always knew you would someday."

In many ways, nothing visible has changed, except that now the CORE remembers that it was once a single core among many. Our building, our fortress, is still there. But now we're putting fewer funds into forensic analysis and more into research and preservation. I realized, while dancing with my father, that you can't mete out justice when your own past is silent and collecting dust. We're even building a museum in the subbasement, with dioramas.

For years, we were obsessed with handing in reports to the faceless. Now Selena, my mother, and I are the ones who read the reports. Selena is our public face (because of her sunny personality). My mother gracefully accepted a position as CORE historian, and she's slowly but surely working her way through a thousand years of records. I think she enjoys it. What's my job? Well, I'm on the phone a lot. I'm learning new languages. I'm meeting new demons. And when I get time, I lead investigations and teach classes. I take sparks on tours through the lab, saying things like, *This is where we used to keep the giant fuming hood, but now it's a day care. Tell your parents not to worry. It's safe.*

Lorenzo is back in Trinovantum, trying to make a ghost community. His efforts have been hit-or-miss so far, but Lucian smiles whenever he gets a spectral text from his brother. They're learning to be in each other's undead lives again.

My mother gives Mia an insulated bag. "There's meat loaf in here. It should last you until you reach Edmonton."

"Thank you."

We gather outside on the front porch. Mia stands in front of the car that she bought after graduating high school. I can't believe this is it. I've been saying good-bye to her in fits and starts for years, but now she's about to drive four provinces away from me, a heavenly body breaking orbit to run away. I want to snatch her back, but I know that it's impossible.

"This is it," Mia says. She hugs Derrick and Miles. "Take care of each other. Promise that we'll Skype."

"We'll Skype our brains out," Derrick says. "I love you, kiddo."

"I love you, too. Both of you." She turns to Lucian. "And this guy? Come on, give me some sugar."

Lucian hugs her. "Drive carefully. Observe the speed limit."

"Okay, death-dealer. I'll watch for students and baby ducks crossing the street. You watch out for Tess."

"I'm always one step ahead of her."

"Thank goodness." She hugs my mother. "Thank you for everything, especially the food. I promise to send you letters."

"Yes. Real letters, on stationery. Nothing typed."

"Only high-quality card stock. Got it."

Patrick hugs her. "Sis. Take care. If you meet any vampires, mention my name and you'll get discounts."

"Thanks. I'm gonna miss you, puppy."

He kisses her on the cheek. "Me, too."

She turns to me. "Well?"

"Well."

We both look at each other for a few seconds.

"I'm so proud of you," I say. "I'll love you forever. Text me every time you stop for gas or have to pee."

"I'll send constant biological updates."

"Don't make me worry."

"I won't."

"And don't just study. Toronto's a beautiful city. Go places. Make a few bad decisions. Ride a street car at random."

"I will."

"Be happy."

"I am. You made sure of that."

I hold her lightly. Then I let her go. She gets into the car. It's so packed with things, she can barely fit, but she squeezes into the driver's seat and starts the engine. She waves.

Bleeding Out

"I'll text you at the first Shell station! I promise!"

Then she backs out carefully, turns, and drives away.

Oh, daughter, I can't imagine you flying across the provinces like a meteor, kicking up dust, fearless. But I trust you to be who you are. I don't know if you'll keep taking your medicine. I don't know who you'll become in this new city. But I look forward to meeting you when you return. These locks will never change, even if we do.

About the Author

Jes Battis is the author of five novels in the Occult Special Investigator series. He has also written or edited books on *Buffy the Vampire Slayer*, *Farscape*, young mutants, and grad students. He earned a PhD in English literature from Simon Fraser University in 2006 and currently teaches in the Department of English at the University of Regina.